ANANGEL ON MAIN STREET

OTHER BOOKS AND AUDIO BOOKS
BY KATHI ORAM PETERSON:

The Forgotten Warrior

AN ANGEL ON MAIN STREET

KATHI ORAM PETERSON

Covenant Communications, Inc.

Cover image: *Shovel the Sidewalk* © Picketfence. Courtesy of iStockphoto.com

Cover design copyrighted 2009 by Covenant Communications, Inc.

Published by Covenant Communications, Inc.
American Fork, Utah

Printed in Canada
First Printing: October 2009

16 15 14 13 12 11 10 09   10 9 8 7 6 5 4 3 2 1

ISBN-13 978-1-59811-721-9
ISBN-10 1-59811-721-1

For John Lyle Oram, my father,
who watches over me from above.

ACKNOWLEDGMENTS

I would like to express my gratitude to my fabulous writing group: The Wasatch Mountain Fiction Writers. Several of us have been meeting once a week and critiquing each other's work for over twenty years. I especially want to give a heartfelt thank-you to my dear friend and fellow writer Dorothy Canada. Her encouragement kept me working on this Christmas story.

I deeply appreciate Covenant Communications believing in my work. A big thank you goes to their staff and especially to my editor, Noelle Perner.

And, as always, I thank my family: Bruce, Ben, Tricia, Kris, Greg, and William.

CONTENTS

FRIED ALLEY CAT

December 22, 1953

I blew into my cold fist as I dodged out of the way of a two-door, hardtop Studebaker. It was a '53 and looked like it had all the bells and whistles—that's what Dad would have said, anyway. He had always wanted a Studebaker, the 1950 bullet-nose Land Cruiser to be exact. Before he went away, he'd confided in me during one of our father and son chats that someday he was going to up and surprise Mom by buying one. I sighed as I watched the automobile maneuver down the snowy alleyway behind Kora's Kountry Kitchen. A lone streetlight blinked on . . . and I realized I was late.

Again.

Mom's imagination would have me finding trouble. I'd promised her that here in Bolton, Idaho, I'd be a good son. And I had every intention of keeping that promise. I was late because I'd stayed after school to clean the chalkboards for Miss White. She couldn't pay much, but I was hopeful I'd earn enough to buy Christmas gifts for my mother and little sister. Plus, working helped keep me out of that trouble I'd promised to avoid. I planned to lie low in this small town and make my mom proud. After all she'd been through, she deserved some happiness.

The snow was about a foot deep in the alley, so I walked in the tire tracks, trying to keep my damp sneakers from becoming even soggier.

"Come on, be lucky, lucky, lucky."

The voice came from beneath the wooden stairs that led to the second-floor back entrance of my apartment. It sounded like my new friend, Horace Fellows. Before school had let out for the day, I'd heard that Ledge Larken and Hammerhead Wilson were trying to convince Horace to shoot craps with them. As soon as I could, I'd taken Horace aside and made him promise me he wouldn't get trapped into a game. But it sounded like he'd ignored my warning. Despite knowing I should go home, I crept around the stairs to see for myself.

I shoved my hands into my dad's worn denim jacket. Though the coat wasn't very warm, it made me feel as though Dad was with me—plus Mom said it made me look like a young James Dean. Peering under the dark stairwell, I saw Horace, and beside him were Ledge and Hammerhead. Horace was pink with hope as he shook his hand. I heard the clinking of dice.

"Don't drop that!" I said, and Horace stopped mid-shake. His chubby stomach pulled at each buttonhole, straining the seams of his red plaid jacket. Guilt smeared a red flush over his freckled face.

I glared at Ledge. He was thirteen, two years older than Horace and me, and was supposed to be Horace's "good" friend. The problem was, good friends didn't rope their buddies into playing dice. I know, because when I lived in Boise, my troubles started with shooting dice. Wanting to earn money to help Mom, I tried to play the game. But the only thing I managed to earn were her tears when she came to pick me up at the police station.

Ledge's pimply face creased into a grin, reminding me of the boys in Boise and the money I'd lost. Hammerhead stood quietly by. His body was built like a buffalo's—large head, massive shoulders. I'd heard plenty of rumors about him. Some kids said that even though he was only thirteen, he could bend metal with his bare hands.

Ledge tugged on his coat sleeves, which left a good one-inch gap of skin above his gloves. He ignored me, staring at Horace. Hammerhead grunted. "Drop 'em, or I'll win automatically."

Horace peered at me for guidance.

"Do it," Ledge commanded.

Rattled, Horace dropped the dice. Two ones. He turned to Ledge and asked, "What does that mean, huh? Did I win? Did you lose? What?"

"It's snake eyes, you dope. I win." Hammerhead held out his beefy hand. "Now pay up."

Horace dug in his pockets while his nervous eyes panned the area as if in search of an escape route.

"You do have it, don't you?" Ledge glared at Horace. "You told me you did. It's only a buck—you've got a buck. At least you did before we stopped at the candy store." Ledge stole a nervous glance at Hammerhead.

I knew Horace had spent his money. My fingers rubbed against the coins in my pocket. Mom had given me some of the money to buy milk for Annie, and the rest was what Miss White had paid me. All totaled, I had a dollar. I knew I should walk away, let Horace get what he deserved, but I couldn't do that, not to a new friend in a new town where I needed to stay out of trouble.

I pulled the money from my pocket and tossed the coins on the frozen ground near the dice.

"Double or nothing? You can win it all back," Ledge said eagerly, his voice cracking.

"No!" I glared at Ledge and then Horace as I tried to warn him that this was a no-win situation.

Hammerhead scooped up the money and lumbered away without even a "thank-you" or "see you later."

"Pa will be looking for me anyways." Horace gave me a grateful look. And though I was glad I'd helped my new friend, I realized what I'd done—taken gifts from my family and, most importantly, milk from my sick little sister.

A shiver made me pull the denim collar of Dad's old coat up near my ears.

Ledge grimaced and glared at me. "Just 'cause you moved here from a big city, don't go thinkin' you can take my friend away from me." He tried to stare me down.

Horace wiped his nose on the back of his hand. "Leave him alone."

I glanced at the wood-slatted stairs over our heads, knowing I didn't have time to argue with Ledge. I needed to get home—but I couldn't leave until Horace was safely on his way.

The back door to Kora's Kountry Kitchen swung open. Light and voices spilled into the alley. We crouched lower into the shadows beneath the stairs. Shooting craps was illegal, and even though I had nothing to do with this game, I didn't want anyone catching me at the scene of the crime.

"Sheriff Anderson, I know no *alley cats* carried off two cases of my top sirloin. Now, you've got to do something about this." Miss Kora's red hair was twisted on top of her head like a beehive, and sprinkled through the hive were tiny specks of golden glitter. A spit curl seemed glued to each of her cheeks. I'd heard she dressed up for every holiday. In February she wore pink heart earrings and silver sequins in her hair; on the Fourth of July she wore star earrings and red-white-and-blue ribbons. Now her Christmas-bell earrings dangled by her neck and flipped back and forth every time she moved her head.

Sheriff Anderson took his time walking around Kora's back door, studying the lock, testing the doorknob, and touching the frame. His big leather boots crunched in the snow as he moved closer to where Ledge, Horace, and I were hiding.

The sheriff stopped in front of the stairs, though his back was to us. He stood there for a long time studying the restaurant. Then he tugged his sheriff-cowboy hat more snuggly on his head. "Well, there are plenty of footprints, but I don't see any cat tracks," he joked as he eyed the door. "Doesn't look like there's been a forced entry."

Zipping up his winter policeman's jacket with star emblems sewn on the sleeves, Sheriff Anderson rubbed his leather-gloved hand over his chin. "Nobody steals in Bolton unless they're starving; then again, if they're hungry, all they have to do is go to the church. Are you sure that meat is missing? Maybe you misplaced it somewhere."

"Sure, I'm always misplacing two cases of prime beef," Miss Kora said, then added, "Do we have to stand in the cold, or did you bring me out here on purpose to warm me up?" She cozied up next to the sheriff.

He stepped away.

"Oh, come on, I could really melt your icicles if you'd let me." She stepped closer to him.

I couldn't believe it. She was going to kiss him right here in front of us.

Holy smokes!

I bit my lips together, but when I looked at Horace and Ledge, all three of us burst out in nervous laughter.

Miss Kora swung around and peered under the stairs. "What are you hoodlums doin' under there?"

Sheriff Anderson peered down at us as well.

At that moment, I saw the dice on the ground. Horace was closest, but he had no idea the trouble he would be in if the sheriff saw them. Ledge was on the other side of me. No way could he scoop up the dice before they were seen.

As fast as I could, I grabbed them.

"What do you have there?" The lawful grip of Sheriff Anderson latched onto my wrist. His voice was stern but soft enough that only I could hear it.

With the sheriff's full attention on me, Horace and Ledge took off, like mice being chased by a tomcat. They nearly ran over Miss Kora, and they never looked back. Trapped, I could only watch them disappear into the night.

What had just happened?

I was going to stay out of trouble. I'd only been trying to help a friend, and now . . . now everything was all messed up.

"Is that you, Micah Connors?" Miss Kora stared at me. "No wonder your momma's late again. You ought to be ashamed of yourself." She popped her gum. "What were you doing under there anyway? Plotting to steal some meat?"

My heart pounded clear up my throat as a tidal wave of fear washed over me.

"Let's not jump to conclusions. Did you say his name is Micah Connors?" Sheriff Anderson slipped the dice from my fingers without Miss Kora seeing and put them in his pocket.

I was confused. Why didn't he show Miss Kora the dice? Why did he put them in his pocket? Other cops I'd dealt with would've come right out and told the world what they'd just found.

"That's his name all right." Miss Kora rubbed her shivering hands over her bare, blue-splotched arms, fighting the cold. "Jiminy, it's cold." She noticed the sheriff was waiting for her to tell him more. "While you were out of town, him, his momma, and his little sister moved into my upstairs apartment. His daddy died fightin' in Korea, and his poor momma tried to find a job in this *won-der-ful* town where no one steals. She couldn't find no work. The rent was due, so

I told her to come waitress for me, but she's been late most every day 'cause of this little poop. He's supposed to be home babysittin' his sick sister."

"Well, Mr. Connors, sounds like you need an escort home. I'll see he gets there, Kora. You go on in and make sure you lock that back door." The sheriff smiled.

Miss Kora rubbed her palms together. "If meat keeps disappearin' I'll have to fry up some of those alley cats you seem so fond of." She smiled at the sheriff and hurried inside.

At that moment, I'd just as soon have become a fried alley cat as face the law . . . and my mother. I slowly lifted my eyes to look at the sheriff, the weight of the world riding my shoulders. What was this man going to do? And what was I going to tell my mom? After everything I'd put her through, she'd never believe I wasn't playing again.

The sheriff straightened to his skyscraper height. My eyes trailed up his tall, lean frame. He was a Goliath. Feeling like a shrimp, I wet my lips and tried to swallow the prickly thorn of trouble stuck in my throat.

The sheriff glowered down at me. "Now, why don't you explain what you boys were doing under there?"

BRIGHT BEAMS

"It's like, uh . . . you see, I . . ." What could I say? How could I deny playing when I'd been caught red-handed? But I had no intention of confessing to something I hadn't done. My future looked bleak. "What are you going to do?" I finally asked and stuffed my hands into my coat pockets.

"I have several options." The sheriff folded his arms. "It all depends on what you were doing under the stairs."

"Those boys were playing a game." I kicked at the snow. "That's all. Just some kids playing a game. I found them and tried to get Horace to go home—then you came out. Is there something wrong with that?" I hoped telling the truth would count for something.

"And you weren't playing—you just happened to have the dice in your hand." The sheriff waited for me to reply. His patience spent, he said, "If you were shooting craps—gambling—do you know what that means?"

I knew all too well, but I wasn't about to let on to him. I shrugged my shoulders, trying to act clueless.

"Give it up, kid." The sheriff took the dice out of his pocket. "See, what I have here is evidence that you are guilty of gambling. Gambling at your age is illegal. So, I can either put you in jail or tell your mom. What will it be?"

I didn't know what to say. My mom had enough problems with Annie's sickness. No way did I want her to know about this. Inhaling a deep, frustrated breath, I blew it out and said, "Jail."

"Interesting . . ." The sheriff clicked his tongue, shaking his head. He returned the dice to his coat pocket. "You know anything about some top sirloin missing from Miss Kora's? As of this moment, you're my number one suspect."

"No, sir! You've gotta believe me. I may have played a few dice games, but that was in my old life—not here! And I've never, ever stolen." My knees felt like they were about to give way. They always acted up when I found myself in a jam.

A broad smile broke over Sheriff Anderson's stone face. He started walking through the snow, down the alleyway toward the front entrance of my apartment. "You *were* shooting craps. No jail for you. We're telling your mom."

"Please," I begged. "I promised her I wouldn't play in this town, and I haven't! You have to believe me, please." He kept walking. I had to say something to make him stop. "It's almost Christmas, and Ma's been working so hard; I just can't disappoint her." My wet tennis shoes were like skates as I tried to keep up with the man who held my fate in his oversized hands.

Sliding around the corner to Main Street, where the street lights shone down on us, I ran smack into someone. Scraggly gray hair poked out below the rim of the old tramp's knit ski cap and hung all the way to the middle of his back.

The old guy's arms flailed as he tried to regain his balance. Something dropped to the ground. I watched as the tramp quickly scrambled to pick up an empty bottle and put it back in his pocket.

"Are you all right, Wolfgang?" Sheriff Anderson knelt beside him. "Haven't been celebrating early, have you?"

"Oh, no, sir. This here's a soda-pop bottle. Just didn't see you two comin', Sheriff. Guess I need to be more careful." His soiled and tattered overcoat looked too heavy for his slumped shoulders.

Wolfgang stood. He was only a foot away from me, and I wished it were farther. His breath smelled of onions and garlic. His square face smiled on me, revealing gaping, brown teeth. When I didn't smile back, the old man's grin turned upside down.

"You need anything?" Sheriff Anderson patted the tramp on his back. "Food? Money?"

"Dadgummit, I'm fine." Wolfgang blushed. "You wouldn't believe the treasures people throw away at the dump." He patted his pocket. "Even pop bottles are worth money."

With the sheriff occupied, I thought I could make my escape. Two more steps, one more step, and I would be out of sight.

"Mr. Connors! It's not good manners to sneak off when you're being escorted home." Sheriff Anderson hadn't turned to look at me, but I knew if I took one more step I'd be going home in cuffs.

"Looks like you're busy, Sheriff." Wolfgang wandered down the alleyway, heading toward Miss Kora's trash barrels. "Be seeing you around." He began rummaging through the garbage.

Sheriff Anderson walked past me, heading down the freshly shoveled sidewalk of Main Street. I followed, my head hung low.

The entrance to the front stairs leading up to my apartment was between Kora's Kountry Kitchen and the Pharaoh Theater. The billboard read, "*Shane,* starring Alan Ladd, Jean Arthur, and Van Heflin." I really wanted to see that movie. But the tickets cost too much.

Mr. Domingo, the owner of the theater, was bent over his shovel as he scooped snow from the walks. His once-tall body was stooped, his face crinkled like worn leather. I had occasionally said hello in hopes that if I were friendly to him, he might someday give me a free movie pass.

The sheriff stopped and leaned over to say quietly, "Tell you what, kid. I won't make you fess up to your mom. I won't even throw you in jail if you'll work off your crime."

"How?" I asked warily.

"For the rest of December, I want you to shovel off Mr. Domingo's and Miss Kora's sidewalks, each and every morning it snows."

"What!" My mouth dropped open.

"Lower your voice, young man." The sheriff's steely gaze cut my protest short. "You want to talk to your mom?" He started for the door leading to my apartment.

Desperate to stop him, I shouted, "All right, you win!"

The sheriff halted.

I tried to think of a way to turn this in my favor. "I'll do it, but don't I get paid something? I mean, that's a lot of work."

"No money—in fact, you're not to tell anyone you shoveled the snow."

"What!"

"Your voice again, Mr. Connors." The sheriff's right eyebrow rose upward. "I want you to pretend to be one of Santa's little helpers. You rise and shine bright and early and get your caboose downstairs shoveling." He rubbed his chin thoughtfully and then continued. "I'll be watching. You blow it, and your mom and I have a talk."

This man was serious. My shoulders slumped. Now, on top of staying up late to watch over Annie, I'd have to get up early and shovel snow—*for free*. I didn't mind watching my little sister—she had always been and would always be special to me—but I still wasn't ready to accept my undeserved punishment.

There had to be a way out of this. Grasping at threads of ideas, I finally thought of something. "You know, this was a really good idea and all, but, you see, I don't have a snow shovel."

"I'll bring the shovel, you show up." Sheriff Anderson opened the door to my building.

"You're going to watch me work?" I couldn't move. What was the matter with this guy? Didn't he have some speeders to catch, some bank robberies to stop?

"I'm at Kora's every morning for breakfast around six thirty. I'll come an hour early, just for you." He motioned for me to go inside.

I stood my ground. "You're not my boss."

"I'm the keeper of law and order, and you broke the law. So that makes me your boss, at least for the rest of the month." He motioned with his gloved hand, directing me into the building. "Come on. I told Miss Kora I'd see you home."

I closed my eyes. Being punished for something I didn't do was so unfair. Then I thought of the many times I hadn't been caught. My gaze slowly climbed up the towering man standing in front of me. I shrugged.

Before I could take a step, the clank of Mr. Domingo's shovel hitting the ground drew our attention.

Shuffling down the sidewalk to the stoplight, the old man shouted, "Look, Sheriff, there in the intersection. What is that?"

Dark against the snow, some type of shack had been constructed on the island in the intersection. Stranger still, there seemed to be a light coming from within. At first I thought a few last rays of sunlight were bouncing off snow crystals. But this light was far too bright; it shone through the cracks of the building, drawing people's attention.

Sheriff Anderson forgot me and followed the old, bent man. I couldn't help but trail after them.

Curious onlookers spilled out of Miss Kora's and Gandy's Gas 'N Pump. Even President Wellington of the First National Bank was drawn out to look at the island. The bright beams faded as more people crowded the area.

The sheriff glanced at the planked walls. The roof was as high as his chest. President Wellington rubbed his nose, and his right eye twitched. Miss Kora looked from person to person, her Christmas bell earrings swaying from side to side.

"What is it?" asked Mr. Domingo.

It was obvious what it was. Without thinking, I blurted, "A stable—you know, like in Bible pictures."

The adults stopped and stared at me, the presumptuous new kid.

"Of course! After all, it is Christmas." Sheriff Anderson stepped beside me.

"The question is, Sheriff—" President Wellington sniffed and tried to stop his eye from twitching, then continued, "—who authorized it? This was not brought up in town council meeting. I hope whoever is doing this does not expect the bank to foot the bill."

A buzz of frustrated chatter hummed through the crowd.

Finally, Sheriff Anderson said, "Maybe it's a gift. Let's wait and see what happens. Come on, folks, break it up."

"But what about the light that was shining?" I asked, curious to know where it had come from. "It's gone now, but that's what brought us here."

Everyone stopped and waited for the sheriff's answer.

"Probably just an oncoming car. Let's be on our way." Anderson motioned for everyone to leave.

People slowly abandoned the area.

I stared at the sadly built structure. The beams of light had been shining from the inside—I was sure of it. Car headlights couldn't do that. Something magical had happened here, and yet the only evidence that remained was a sad-looking replica of a stable.

"Mr. Connors." Sheriff Anderson's voice. "I need to take you home."

I gritted my teeth and followed him.

THE BLACK PIT

I stuffed my fists in the pockets of my dad's jacket and led the way. Before we reached the entrance leading to my apartment, however, Sheriff Anderson stopped. "You surprise me, Micah. I didn't have you pegged as a Bible studier."

"I don't study the Bible!" I clenched my teeth. It would be better to be known as a craps shooter than a Bible studier.

"You just look at the pictures?" Like a dentist's drill, the sheriff's words were getting a little too close to a nerve.

"My mother reads the book a lot, okay?" How could I tell this nosey know-it-all that since my father had died, my mother was forever quoting verses? Our whole lives were centered on stories from that book—a book filled with fables and false hopes.

Swinging open the door to the building, I said, "I live at the top of the stairs, so you've done what you told Miss Kora you would do."

I hoped I'd convinced the sheriff to leave. The last thing I needed was this man barging into my home, poking around, and maybe telling my mom what he thought had happened in back of the Kountry Kitchen. I wanted Mom to know on my terms, because for sure and certain she'd hear about it from Miss Kora. But I needed to ease her into the subject without the sheriff standing over my shoulder.

"Mr. Connors, I wouldn't want you to get lost between here—" Sheriff Anderson pointed from the last stair to the top "—and there."

I started up the dimly lit staircase. With each step, I wondered what I could do or say that would lessen the damage Mr. I'm-the-king-of-Bunker-Hill Sheriff could cause.

Nearing the door, I hesitated. A sad, hollow emptiness filled me. It did every time I returned home, knowing my father wasn't there. Since he'd been gone, I had the responsibility of taking care of Mom and my sister. I hated the thought of letting the sheriff see what a poor job I had done.

Feeling the tall man's presence behind me, I sucked in a deep breath and pushed open the door. As I walked in and took off my coat, I realized the kitchen was almost as cold as it was outside. I glanced around. The bleak, yellowed walls were bare of cheery pictures, although the room was spotlessly clean. A table flanked with mismatched throw-away chairs held a cup with a pink plastic tulip in it—the only happy color in the room. My cot was in the corner with my box of clothes stored underneath. I tossed my coat on the bed.

"Micah, is that you?" Mom's hopeful voice called to me from her bedroom.

"Yeah, Mom."

"Where have you been? I've been waiting for you. I'm late." Mom raced into the kitchen dressed in her red, gingham-checked waitress uniform. Her cinnamon-colored hair was twisted into a knot. She abruptly stopped when she saw the sheriff with me. "Micah?"

"Uh, Mom . . ." I hated seeing the fear in her eyes. "This is Sheriff Anderson." I crossed my fingers behind me, hoping the sheriff would keep his word and not tell her what had happened.

I looked up at him. The sheriff's stern face had changed. His eyes were sparkly. What was the matter with this guy? Not a minute ago he'd been acting tough enough to eat rusty nails with his eggs. Now, he was actually . . . smiling.

Finally, Sheriff Anderson cleared his throat. "I ran into Micah at Miss Kora's. Thought I'd see him home. You folks are new in town."

All at once the sheriff seemed to realize he still wore his hat. He pulled it from his head. His straw-colored hair was matted to his forehead where the hat rim had been pressed.

"Yes, we moved here less than a month ago. I'm Dawn Connors. Did Micah do something wrong?" Without thinking, Mom started to sit where there wasn't a chair. Quickly, I grabbed a stool and caught her without her noticing.

"No, ma'am. Micah and I hit it right off." Astonished, I blinked several times and pinched myself to make sure I wasn't dreaming. I looked from the sheriff to my mother, then back to the sheriff. Did he like Mom? Stranger things had happened. Sheriff Anderson kept watching her like she was a triple-decker hot fudge sundae.

"I wanted to welcome you to town," he finally said. "We're friendly folks here."

Because the sheriff was obviously keeping his word and not telling my mom what he thought I'd done, I decided this would be a good time to sneak off and check on my little sister. I escaped into the living room—Annie's room.

Here she could gaze out the window and watch the traffic and people. I walked quietly to the bed, hoping not to wake her. But she was already awake. Her white-blond hair hung limply around her face. Her chocolate-colored eyes, which used to shine, were red-rimmed and bloodshot. "Hi, Micah. Did you bring me a treat?"

What I wanted to bring her was a game called Buzzer. I'd seen it in Jefferson's Hardware Store, and right away I had known she would love it. Annie liked puzzle games, and Buzzer was a maze. A little bee with an iron weight in its body was supposed to follow the player's magnetic stick. The trick was to drag the bee through a maze of honeycomb.

"Not today, Annie Bananie." I plopped down on the side of her bed.

"You promised you wouldn't call me that anymore." Her pink bottom lip curled into a pout.

"You know you like it." I tweaked her short nose.

"Who is Mama talking to?" Annie whispered.

Before I could answer, the sheriff and Mom stepped into the room. The sheriff ducked so he wouldn't bump his head on the top of the doorframe.

"Annie, this is Sheriff Anderson. He stopped by to meet us." Mom smoothed Annie's hair away from her face.

Annie turned on her charm with a brilliant smile. "I saw you on the island in the street. What's out there?"

"Micah thinks it's a stable." The sheriff clutched the brim of his hat. "Like the one in the Bible."

"Really!" Annie's eyes grew wide. "A real stable?"

"Yep, that's what it looks like." Sheriff Anderson smiled at Annie and then glanced around the room.

I followed his gaze. The solid oak rocker Dad had built for Mom sat in the corner. Two dilapidated folding chairs leaned against the wall. The scarred and warped card table next to Annie's bed held a radio, a pitcher of water, some chipped cups, a couple of bottles of medicine, and Mom's Bible.

Then it hit me like a kick to the stomach: The sheriff saw our poor furniture and felt sorry for us. Who did he think he was, feeling sorry for *my* family? Our furniture might not add up to much, but Mom had to sell most of the good stuff to pay Annie's doctor bills.

"Sheriff, I hate to cut your visit short, but I'm late for work, and Miss Kora's been so nice, giving me a job and all." My mom tugged on her worn sweater and slung her shoulder-strap purse over her arm.

"Don't you have a coat, Mrs. Connors?" The sheriff's eyebrows pulled together as his face filled with concern. "It's really cold out there."

Who did this man think he was? I took care of Mom. What did he think he was doing, butting into our lives, nosing in where he had no business, and then feeling sorry for us?

It was one thing for the sheriff to like Mom enough to forget the dice game but quite another for him to edge in on my responsibilities as man of the house.

"Call me Dawn." Mom smiled. "I'll be fine, Sheriff. I'm just going downstairs to the restaurant. You really must stop by another time when we can visit." She placed her hands on my shoulders.

I grinned at the sheriff as if to say, "So there, she's my mother, and you leave her alone."

"Please call me Garth." Sheriff Anderson ignored me. "I'll walk you down." He held his arm out for her to take.

She fell for it and placed her hand in the crook of the sheriff's massive arm.

Before leaving, the sheriff bowed to Annie. "Nice meeting you, Miss Annie. Here, I have something for you." He pulled a Hershey's candy bar from his coat pocket. Annie's eyes sparkled with excitement. Then the sheriff turned to me. "It's supposed to snow in the morning." He winked.

Mom stopped, studied me, and then the sheriff. A puzzled wariness flushed over her as she said, "Would you wait for me in the kitchen, Sheriff? I need to speak with my son."

Sheriff Anderson disappeared through the room's entryway.

"Micah, is there something you need to tell me about the sheriff's visit?" Mom stood still, waiting for my reply.

She was already late, and the sheriff was waiting for her. This was not how I wanted to tell Mom about the trouble with the dice game. But if I didn't tell her, Miss Kora would . . . or maybe not. Sometimes she left before the night shift came to work. And Mom was late, so the chances of Miss Kora being gone were very good. And there was no sense getting Mom all upset before she went to work. I could tell her in the morning or sometime tomorrow. Looking up at Mom, I answered, "It's like the sheriff said. He wanted to meet you."

And that was the truth . . . well, part of it.

"Okay then." The worry lines on Mom's forehead relaxed. "There's a can of peaches in the fridge, and there's the milk you bought. You put it away when you came in, didn't you?" She looked at me, and I nodded. She continued. "Bread's in the cupboard. I'll see if there's anything I can bring up later. Be good." She kissed me on the cheek.

I couldn't tell Mom there was no milk. No milk for Annie. I bit my lip. I felt like slime. How could I have given Mom's hard-earned money to help Horace? At the time, it had felt like the right thing to do, and I had been sure Mom would agree. But right now everything was so mixed up. That trouble I'd been determined not to find had reached out and grabbed me good.

Mom left without looking back. I waited, listening for the door to close before I turned to Annie with the grim news of no milk. I didn't know how I would tell her. Guilt pushed me toward my little sister.

Before I could say anything, Annie handed me the candy bar and said, "Is it really a stable?"

"Don't you want the chocolate?" My stomach growled.

She shook her head.

Annie handing me her candy made me feel even more rotten about losing the milk money. Again my stomach growled. I'd make it up to my little sister tomorrow. Tomorrow I'd find a way to buy some milk—I could ask Miss White for an advance. That's it! Everything would work out, so there was no reason I couldn't enjoy this candy bar right now.

Yet, as I eagerly peeled the foil paper and dropped the wrappings in the garbage, I couldn't take a bite. Setting the chocolate on the card table, hoping Annie would eat it instead, I said, "Yeah, well, it looks like a stable to me."

"Do you know what this means?" Her eyes danced with delight.

"No." I shrugged. "Just that somebody is fixing up the town for Christmas."

"It's more." She pursed her lips together as though in deep thought. "Nobody knows, do they?"

"What do you mean, nobody knows?" I asked, puzzled.

"Nobody knows where it came from." Annie struggled to plump up her pillows.

"No, nobody knows. Why?" I helped her.

"An angel is building it." She snuggled down in her bed.

"There's no such things as angels," I said.

"They're in the Bible. And Mama says the Bible is true. Besides, I prayed that Jesus would come and make me better. The stable means He's coming, Micah. You wait and see."

I gazed at my little sister. Surely she knew that if someone was indeed planning a Nativity scene that the people in the Nativity would be fake—including the baby Jesus. "Annie, you do understand that the baby Jesus will be a doll, right?" I glanced out the frosted window to the intersection island where the lonely stable stood, then back to my little sister.

"Of course, but Mama said prayer makes miracles possible." Annie yawned, then blinked her hope-filled eyes and continued. "Don't you see, Micah? Jesus will be there no matter if there's a doll or not. I just know it. Sometimes, when I'm feelin' really sick, the room gets quiet, and I think I'm dyin'." She rubbed her nose and looked up at me. "That's when I feel my heart poundin' and I know I'm still here. Feelin' my heart means God's watchin' over me." She closed her eyes. "Everything is gonna be all right," she mumbled as she drifted off.

I pressed my forehead against the cold window. After my father died, Annie had become sick. She'd started running a high fever, and

Mom had taken her to the hospital. They told us that Annie had rheumatic fever and that it made her heart weak. The doctors could do nothing. Annie had grown weaker and weaker.

In the back of my mind, I knew she might die. I tried not to think about it too much. Death was a black pit that sucked people in and never let them out. I couldn't stand the thought of Annie dying and slipping into that hole—that nothingness—like our father.

My mind flashed back to the day Dad left for Korea. He was dressed in his uniform, smiling as he waved good-bye. I had prayed every night that he'd be protected from harm. But prayer hadn't stopped him from being killed. And even though my father was dead, my mom still believed in prayer. Her belief made her strong most of the time, but sometimes, late at night, I could hear her crying.

Now, staring at the window pane, I saw the Bible reflected in the glass. I shook my head and looked away. The book was filled with stories that gave my mom and Annie false hope. Jesus was just another story, another fairy tale.

But Annie believed the fairy tale.

If seeing the baby Jesus doll would make her feel like her prayers had been heard, I had to find who was building the Nativity and borrow that doll. Maybe, with Annie's faith in miracles, she would be cured just by holding it. I gazed at my little sister. Her breathing was shallow, barely making her chest move.

Fear prickled up my spine, and I knew I had to find the baby Jesus before time ran out.

A COUPLE OF SHEEP

December 23, 1953

Bzzzzzzzzzz. My hand slowly emerged from under the blankets. After slapping the floor several times, I finally made contact with the alarm clock. Pulling it under the covers with me, I shut it off and tried to see the time in the illuminated hands. Five thirty. No one in their right mind got up at five thirty to shovel snow off sidewalks for free.

No one except me and that blasted sheriff who was full of beans.

Poking my head and arm from beneath the covers, I reached under the cot and tugged out my cardboard box of clothes. Trying to focus on pants and a shirt, I realized my mouth tasted like the inside of a dirty sneaker.

I sat up, shook my head, and ran my fingers through my hair, mumbling, "I don't want to do this." Yearning to lie down, I stared back at my inviting pillow. A vision of Sheriff Anderson knocking on the door at six o'clock made me flip back the covers.

I jerked on a pair of holey jeans and a striped T-shirt, stuffed my feet into socks and shoes, then yanked on my jacket . . . Dad's jacket. He would have done this without the moaning and groaning, without the sheriff blackmailing him. Dad would have done this because he was a nice guy. All at once, the burden seemed lighter.

Peeking out the frost-coated kitchen window, I saw streetlights reflecting off freshly fallen snow. It had to be sub-zero out there. Maybe if I didn't wash my face I wouldn't wake up enough to feel the chill.

A shudder pushed me out of the apartment. Carefully, I closed the door and quietly tiptoed down the dimly lit stairwell to the front entrance and then out to Main Street.

Parked at the curb was the sheriff's black-and-white Fordor Sedan with the engine still running. I was relieved he didn't have the red bubble-gum light flashing on top. As soon as I stepped from the building, Sheriff Anderson popped out of his car.

"Here you go, Mr. Connors." He handed me a shovel over the hood of the car.

I reached, exposing my bare hands.

"You should have worn gloves."

I should be in bed, I thought as I pulled the shovel from the sheriff's grasp and walked through the powdery snow to the corner of the theater.

"Wait a minute." Sheriff Anderson leaned back into the open doorway of his car, then tossed something at me.

On reflex, I dropped the shovel, catching whatever flew my way. I looked down to see what I was holding and saw . . . gloves. The sheriff's leather, fur-lined gloves. The man felt sorry for me. If he thought I was going to use these, he was crazy.

I raised my arm to fling the gloves back, but the sheriff had already climbed into his warm car and closed the door.

Maybe I'll just use them this morning. I eased my hands into the plush, velvety warmth.

Busying myself, I scooped the snow to the curb. Only two inches had fallen, so it wasn't too bad. My toes were cold, but I ignored them the best I could.

As I finished the sidewalks, the sheriff turned off the patrol car and climbed out.

"Good job. How about I buy you a cup of cocoa when Miss Kora opens?" The sheriff smiled, took the shovel, tapped the clinging snow off the blade, and put it in the trunk. As he did so, an idea came to me. Maybe, if I could get the sheriff to give me the money for the cocoa, I could buy milk for Annie. But I'd have to say just the right words.

"If I go with you, Miss Kora might figure out I'm the one who did this," I said, hoping the guy would simply toss me a couple of quarters.

"You're probably right." Sheriff Anderson deposited his keys in his pocket, tilted his cowboy hat to the front of his head, and turned toward Miss Kora's door.

This was not the reaction I had been hoping for. I yelled, "Wait!"

"Yes?" The sheriff stopped and slowly turned.

"Your gloves." I pulled them off and reached out to pass them to the sheriff. As I did so, I realized that although I couldn't stand the idea of asking this man for something, I had to—for Annie. Drawing on courage, I looked him square in the eyes and said, "Could use a carton of milk. Costs the same as a cup of cocoa." I didn't know if that was true or not.

Sheriff Anderson stood there, taking forever to answer. Then, finally, he cleared his throat. "Sure. Let's go over to Gandy's Gas 'N Pump. He opens at five every day for the farmers, even when harvest is over."

I waited outside the store. I didn't want Mr. Gandy to know who the milk was for, so I pretended to look over the Christmas trees that leaned against the front of the building.

One pretty tree had needles that were almost blue. The tag on it read *"Blue Spruce"* in black marker. Peering through the store window, I saw the sheriff talking with Mr. Gandy. The older man was as round as a tire, and his white beard reminded me of Santa Claus. All he needed was a red suit and maybe some more white hair on top of his balding head.

Could Mr. Gandy be the one building the Nativity? He could have sneaked over to the island without being seen. Thinking of the Nativity, I turned to look at it just as Sheriff Anderson walked out of the store with the carton of milk.

The red stoplight flashed as my eyes rested on the little stable. During the night, something had been added. The sheriff saw it at the same time I did. I wondered why I hadn't noticed before, but then I remembered that when I'd first come outside to do my good deed, it had been darker, and I'd been half asleep.

The sheriff and I crossed the street together. As we approached the scene, he said, "Isn't this something?"

I watched as he squatted to examine the figures—which appeared to be sheep. A wool-like fabric covered a couple of wooden sawhorses, and rags underneath the material were tied to the frame. The sheep's wooden heads were bowed before the stable.

Out of the corner of my eye, I saw another figure. "Look, there's a cow, and over there's a donkey."

The other animals had been placed inside the stable and had been made with larger sawhorses. Fur-like hides covered the bulk of the lumber bodies.

"This is wonderful," said the sheriff, holding the carton of milk in one hand and patting the back of the donkey as if it were real.

"Yeah, wonderful . . ." All I could think about was finding who was doing this so I could borrow the baby Jesus and take it to Annie. Maybe the sheriff knew more than he was letting on. "'Preciate the milk, Sheriff," I said as I took the carton from him. "Mr. Gandy is the one who's doin' this, isn't he? He's just across the street."

"No." The sheriff shook his head. "It's not him."

"Sure it is. Who else could it be?"

His eyes locked on me. Finally he said, "Mr. Gandy's wife is an invalid. They live in the back of the station. Between waiting on customers and taking care of her, he barely has time to sleep, let alone build this. Why the curiosity, Mr. Connors?"

"Just wondering." No way was I telling this man what Annie had said about the baby Jesus. He might use Annie's imagination as an excuse to become a permanent fixture around the apartment. I could take care of my sister. I didn't need any help from this snoop.

The lights inside Kora's Kountry Kitchen came on. "Looks like your breakfast will be ready soon." I turned to leave.

"Mr. Connors," said Sheriff Anderson. "You seem pretty interested in this act of kindness someone is doing for the town. I get the feeling you're hiding something. I don't know what you're up to yet, but remember, I'll be keeping my eye on you."

REMEMBER THE ANGELS

As I placed the milk in the fridge, I heard Annie moan. I glanced at the clock and saw that it was a little after six thirty. Mom wasn't up yet. She had worked until well after midnight.

By the refrigerator light, I quickly poured a cup of milk. Shutting the fridge, I tiptoed past Mom's bedroom.

The neon sign from Kora's Kountry Kitchen flashed on and off into the living room. I looked at my little sister, wondering how she could sleep. She lay so still in her bed. I smoothed her hair away from her forehead. Damp curls stuck to her clammy skin.

"Micah." Her voice was a mere whisper.

"Hey, Annie Bananie. Brought you some milk."

"I had a bad dream, Micah." She sat up and took the glass from me. "I dreamed the baby Jesus didn't come. He didn't come in time, and I . . ." Her bottom lip quivered. Tears pooled in her big brown eyes. "You know what this means?" She lay back against her feather pillows, ignoring the milk in the cup.

"That you had a bad dream." I tried to smile.

"No." The word barely slipped from her lips.

I knew what she meant. She thought she was going to die before Christmas. I swallowed back the fear that rose in my throat. She wasn't going to die. She couldn't.

I had to do something, say something so she would quit thinking about this. "It means you ate sauerkraut and marshmallows for dinner. That causes bad dreams, you know."

Annie shook her head, not cracking a smile. Ordinarily my jokes would cheer her up. But it didn't work this time. So I added, "You haven't looked at the island this morning, have you?"

Annie strained to see over the windowsill. "Look! Animals!" She grabbed my arm and blinked. Rubbing her eyes, she looked again. Clearly relieved, Annie sat back on her bed. "Maybe He will come in time." She sipped her milk.

When Annie was finished, I took the cup and placed it on the card table beside us. "I want you to go back to sleep. All you need is rest." I pulled the patchwork quilt up to her chin as she laid her head on her pillow.

"Do you think there'll be shepherds next?" she asked weakly.

"Probably."

"But that won't happen 'til tomorrow, huh?" Her eyes opened wide. "I know what I'll do. Hand me the candy bar wrapper, the shiny one that the Hershey's bar was in."

I retrieved the foil wrapper from the brown garbage sack next to the bed and handed it to Annie, noticing that the candy was still on the card table where I'd left it. Obviously Annie was not going to eat the Hershey's bar. Unable to stand the sight of it because it reminded me of the sheriff, I pushed the chocolate into the garbage.

"I'm going to make baby Jesus a shepherd's staff," Annie said. "One small enough for His little baby hands."

Holding the wrapper, she slumped down in her bed. "Joseph, Mary, and the angels will come too." Annie's eyelids dropped and finally closed. "Remember the angels. They have to be there, then the manger and baby Jesus." Her head lolled to one side as she fell back asleep.

As I gazed out the window at the scene in the intersection, a sinking feeling grew in the pit of my stomach. There were only two days until Christmas. I had to find that baby Jesus today.

SKIPPING SCHOOL

I walked down the alleyway, trudging through snow up the hill to the railroad tracks. I balanced on the rail while scanning the fields of sagebrush and cottonwood trees.

Horace's house was down the tracks a ways. Since we'd become friends, I'd started walking to school with him. Ledge always managed to join us before we reached Bolton Elementary. The junior high Ledge attended was next door. I wondered what my two new friends would say to me today after what had happened last night—especially Ledge. He was a bad influence on Horace. Somehow I needed to help Horace understand that some friends were just trouble. But today, I had other things on my mind. And going to school wasn't one of them. I had some serious snooping around town to do. I had to find out who was building that Nativity before it was too late, and I was going to need some help.

Somehow I had to convince Horace—and maybe Ledge—to skip school. Those two owed me for taking the blame for their game last night. With the three of us searching for the Nativity builder, we were bound to find the baby Jesus.

Breathing in the crisp air, I couldn't help but think about how Annie would have loved walking on the tracks, breathing deeply and feeling alive. Instead she was stuck in bed. I kicked at the snow along the track as I walked.

Finally, Horace's small house came into view. Bright green paint made the building appear larger than it really was.

I slid down the hill and tromped up to the house. As I raised my fist to knock on the door, it swung open. Before me stood Mr. Fellows, his hawklike face glowing red. He stopped short when he saw me planted in front of him.

Mr. Fellows was as tall and skinny as a hockey stick. He wore a red hunter's cap, and the flaps covered his ears. His jacket was the same ugly red plaid as Horace's.

"What do you want?" he growled.

"Came to pick up Horace for school." I hoped this man wouldn't yell at me. For just a moment, I considered the possibility that Mr. Fellows could be the one building the Nativity. Maybe he wasn't always so grouchy. Maybe there was a soft side to Mr. Fellows that he didn't like to show to just anybody.

He stepped back so I could enter the house.

"Have a seat." He pointed to a faded flowered chair that was missing its legs.

"Horace!" Mr. Fellows shouted. "Your friend's here. I'm late." He pulled his well-worn winter gloves on his hands, mumbling as he walked out the door. "Kid makes me late every morning. Don't know why I put up with this family. Things are going to change around here." The door slammed behind him. The windows rattled.

Horace strolled out licking strawberry jam off his plump fingers, not worried at all about his dad. "Hi! Got away from the sheriff, huh?"

"Piece of cake," I said.

"Really? Golly, I thought you were a goner. I mean, he had you by the wrist! And Miss Kora looked like she was going to kick you to the moon." Horace grabbed his coat off the hall coat rack.

"I'm not afraid of Miss Kora or that dumb sheriff." I had more important things to talk about. "Anderson wasn't as mad as your dad was just now."

"Dad starts growling this time every year." Horace tugged on his coat. "He hates Christmas. I mean, he hates Santa Claus—and even the story about Jesus." Horace tried to button his coat over his belly but quickly gave up.

"Then I guess your dad isn't the one building the Nativity in town." I watched my friend struggle to tug his galoshes on over his shoes.

"Nativity? No way. My dad don't got no religion."

* * *

As Horace and I trudged through the snow toward the redbrick school, I tried to think of how I could coax my friend into coming with me. Ledge joined us before I could bring up the subject.

"Anderson let you go, huh?" Ledge asked, avoiding eye contact with me. He knew darned well he should have been the one caught. Well, at least he had a guilty conscience—it would be all the easier to spring my plan on him and Horace. "Yeah, he let me go. Hey guys, you want to play a joke on the whole town?"

"Cool." Ledge smiled as if glad the subject of last night had been dismissed. He flung a snowball at a sparrow on the telephone line. It soared wide of the bird. "What do you have in mind?"

I quickly told them how a Nativity was appearing bit by bit on the town's island intersection. Then I said, "If we find out who's doin' it, we can hide the baby Jesus until after Christmas Day." I couldn't very well tell them the truth—that my little sister needed the doll so she wouldn't die. They would only ask questions about Annie's illness—questions I had no answers to—and then they would feel sorry for me.

I saw a glimmer of excitement in both their eyes.

"Hey, cool idea." Ledge scooped up more snow and began molding another snowball.

"Golly, really?" Whenever Horace got excited, his cheeks turned red as matchstick heads. "You really think we oughtta do this?"

"Sure." Ledge flung another snowball at the bird. The sparrow flew off before the snow splattered on the wire. "This will be fun. As soon as school's over, we'll head for the hardware store." Ledge began walking. "If you want to know anything in this town, you ask Mr. Jefferson. That man can go on and on about everybody's business—and everything you ever wanted to know about nails. Plus, he knows everyone within three counties."

"Why can't we go right now?" I asked, trying to sound casual.

"If we go now, we'll be late for school." Horace scowled as if he'd stepped in dog leavings.

"And the problem is?" I persisted.

"You want to skip school? Not even go?" The light was beginning to turn on for Ledge.

"How can we keep an eye on things and do some snooping if we're in school all day?" I crossed my fingers.

"My dad would kill me dead." Horace's cheeks flamed again. "I mean, you saw how he was this morning. And he didn't even have a reason to be mad."

"Horace's right—his old man would be real mad." Ledge kept walking with Horace by his side. "And I can't have the sheriff pickin' me up for skippin'. We can watch the island after school. Today's a short day for the elementary school and the junior high. That gives us this afternoon and all day Saturday. It can wait."

For a moment, I'd forgotten about Sheriff Anderson. I sure didn't want to run into him again, but helping Annie was more important than school and was worth the risk. "You guys go ahead. I'm going to see what I can find out on my own."

"Good luck!" Ledge waved to me as he and Horace walked away.

So much for friends helping friends—especially after what I'd gone through last night and this morning for them.

I shook my head; I had to forget them. What I needed was a plan. I pictured the town in my mind. Gandy's Gas 'N Pump was on the southwest corner of the intersection. I remembered the sheriff saying that Mr. Gandy had a sick wife and was way too busy to build a Nativity, so I marked him off my mental checklist. The courthouse with the big clock on the front was straight east across Main Street from Gandy's. Judges, lawyers, and accountants worked there.

And so did Sheriff Anderson. But I couldn't picture any of those people building the Nativity . . . especially not the sheriff.

Across the street from the courthouse to the north was the bank. President Wellington couldn't possibly be the one. He was too busy counting money.

Next to the bank was Jefferson's Hardware Store. Mr. Jefferson . . . He was a definite candidate. He would have all the materials to build the Nativity. And if it wasn't him, he'd probably know who it might be. Like Ledge had said, Mr. Jefferson knew everyone. Jefferson's Hardware Store was where I would start my search.

HEART MURMUR

Ding, ding. The bell above Jefferson's Hardware Store's door announced my arrival.

Mr. Jefferson was talking to Farmer Smithers back by the nail barrel. Turning in my direction, he called, "Be with you in a minute." Mr. Jefferson had white bushy sideburns fanning out by the sides of his face; he reminded me of a koala bear I'd seen in a *National Geographic* magazine. His movements were slow and sluggish as well, as if he'd been snacking on eucalyptus leaves.

I knew Mr. Jefferson would take his time. Some kid wasn't as important as Farmer Smithers. Disappointed I couldn't ask about the Nativity, I decided to look around.

Walking down the toy aisle, I realized how odd it was that a hardware store sold toys. Bigger towns like Boise had stores that sold *only* toys. I had never had money to buy any, and Mom hadn't either, but she loved to take me window shopping. She loved the smell of those fresh, clean stores.

Mr. Jefferson's store smelled of tools, old wood, and some kind of oil. The crafty old man had set his toy merchandise up front, near the display window: bright red fire engines, sleek trains, hula hoops, toy ships, and wagons. Walking on, I found myself in front of the games. Mr. Potato Head, Pick-up Sticks, Old Maid cards, Monopoly—and the Buzzer game. I let out a breath and grabbed the game. I wanted to buy this for Annie. She would have so much fun. I wanted to buy her everything in the store.

Suddenly an idea came to me. What I really needed to buy Annie was a doll—a doll that looked like baby Jesus! Filled with hope and still clutching the Buzzer game, I went down several more aisles, searching for such a doll. Barbies, Raggedy Anns, dolls that walked and even some that wet their pants. "Yuck!" I muttered and continued my search. Finally, I saw a doll that could pass as baby Jesus. It had short brown hair, eyes that opened and closed, and—this was the important thing—it was wrapped in a blanket all snugly like a newborn, just like Jesus would have been on Christmas morning.

Ding, ding. Someone else walked into the store. I couldn't see who it was, but I heard Mr. Jefferson say, "Be with you in a minute."

I sighed. With two grown-ups to talk to, Mr. Jefferson would completely forget about me. Using the tip of my finger, I traced the doll's smiling face. This one could work. I turned the baby over, searching for the price tag. Three dollars and ninety-nine cents. It might as well have cost ten or twenty dollars.

But without this doll, Annie might . . .

I quickly glanced up and down the aisle and even behind me. No one was in sight. I set the Buzzer game on a shelf and stuffed the doll up the front of my dad's denim jacket, then quickly crossed my arms. No one would know, and Annie would be so happy.

I turned to walk away but stopped.

Yesterday I'd told the sheriff that I'd never stolen anything before. And now here I was about to steal a doll and then pretend it was baby Jesus. That just wasn't right, even if I didn't believe in Bible stories.

I had never stolen. And I never would.

Besides, I still had a chance to find whoever was building the Nativity. Slowly, I exhaled a long breath and I pulled the doll from under my coat. I set it on top of the Buzzer game.

I thought of my sister, sick and in bed. Taking the doll would have been easy, and Annie would have been happy. Tears clouded my eyes. "It's not fair," I whispered. Clutching my hand into a fist, I hit the Buzzer game the doll lay on. The game and doll fell to the floor.

"Shoot," I mumbled as I crouched to pick up the toys.

"Need some help, Mr. Connors?" Next to the doll, black shiny policemen/cowboy boots stepped into my view of the worn, hardwood floor.

I knew without looking that it was Sheriff Anderson standing over me. "No! How long have you been watching?"

"Long enough." The sheriff squatted next to me. "What is this?" He picked up the doll. "Why would you try to steal a baby doll, then put it back?" He rested his heavy hand on my slumped shoulder.

Looking into Sheriff Anderson's eyes, I could tell he cared, and for a moment I was tempted to tell him about Annie and how scared I was that she might die. I knew I needed help to solve this one.

But help from the sheriff?

I looked away. I needed my father, but he was dead.

I could feel Sheriff Anderson's eyes on me, but I kept my gaze averted. I couldn't count on him. It wouldn't be the same as my dad. I would protect Annie and my mother on my own. I had to be strong. Anger crowded away any feelings of helplessness.

"I wasn't stealin' any doll." I pushed the sheriff's hand away. "I bumped it, and it fell on the floor. Okay?" Standing, I took the baby doll from the sheriff and placed it back on the shelf.

"Then tell me—why you aren't in school? That's where all good little boys should be two days before Christmas." Sheriff Anderson rose to his goalpost height, all traces of sympathy gone. Good. I could deal with him now.

"Got the flu," I said, crossing my fingers and avoiding the sheriff's eyes.

"I see. You have the flu, so you've come to Mr. Jefferson's Hardware Store. You want his medical opinion? You must know a different side of Mr. Jefferson than the rest of the town. Let me get him for you." The sheriff turned, and his holstered gun flashed before my eyes.

"I'm feeling much better now," I called and sprinted past Sheriff Anderson, heading for the front door.

"Wait up. I want to let your mom know how poorly you've been feeling." I looked back and saw that the sheriff had followed me. Great! With his long legs chasing me, there was no sense in running. Besides, he knew where I lived. I didn't know what to do. I sure didn't want to go home dragging the sheriff with me . . . again. Mom would only worry. But right now I had no choice. Maybe I could pretend I really was sick.

My stomach was starting to feel a little upset anyway, I reasoned, as I watched the sheriff approach.

* * *

Trudging up the stairs to the apartment, I could smell something wonderful.

I couldn't quite figure out if it was cookies or bread baking, but whatever it was, I couldn't believe it was coming from my apartment.

"Your mom must be cooking up something good." The sheriff stepped onto the warped wooden landing at the same time I did. "Too bad you have the flu."

"You don't need to come in." My hand rested on the wobbly doorknob.

Sheriff Anderson folded his arms against the stars on his coat sleeves and gave me a think-again look.

Shrugging, I opened the door.

An unfamiliar blue-and-white speckled pot, with soup vapors steaming out of the top, sat on the stove. Freshly baked bread with butter melting down the sides of the golden-brown crust waited on the cracked countertop. A plate of tempting spice cookies filled a chipped plate next to the bread.

My attention turned to the small kitchen table where an unfamiliar black overcoat lay. I heard voices coming from the living room . . . Annie's room.

Adult talking.

Serious adult talking.

Forgetting the sheriff, I followed the voices. An elderly man in a dark suit sat on Annie's bedside. She looked like she was sleeping. The man was obviously a doctor; he was probing over Annie's chest with a stethoscope. Mom stood behind the doctor, biting her knuckle.

Sheriff Anderson had followed me into the room. "Is everything all right?" he asked when he saw the doctor.

"No." Mom fought back tears. She pulled a hankie from her duster pocket.

"Shh, go in the other room." The doctor's bushy eyebrows seemed to rise in an exclamation point. "I'll be with you in a minute."

Sheriff Anderson and I followed my mother to the kitchen. As she walked, her woolly socks dusted the yellowed linoleum floor.

"What happened, Mom?" My voice trembled.

She leaned against the faded wall. The sheriff immediately grabbed a spindly chair from under the table.

"Thanks." Mom's eyes were lined red with worry, her cheeks flushed. She wiped her nose with her hanky. Flipping her long braid over her shoulder, she continued. "Miss Kora brought up this food for our lunch. Wasn't that thoughtful?" A shadow of a smile flickered at her mouth. "After she left, I went in to check Annie and realized she had a fever. I found Doctor Goodman's number in the phonebook and called him from the pay phone in front of the restaurant."

"You should have used Kora's phone. She wouldn't have minded." The sheriff pulled off his cowboy hat, curling the brim with his fingers.

"She's already done so much, and I didn't want to impose. Anyway, the doctor came right over." She turned to look at me. "I'm so glad you're home, son," she said and gave me a hug.

"Mrs. Connors." The worried-looking doctor walked in, pulled the stethoscope from his thick neck, and set his black medical bag on the table next to his overcoat. "She'll sleep for another hour or so. You said she had rheumatic fever about a year ago and never fully recovered?"

My mother nodded.

"I'm sorry to say she's had a bad relapse. This happens sometimes, and it appears she's developed a heart murmur. That little heart of hers is working triple time. Has she seen a doctor for her heart?"

"Yes, in Boise. He said there was nothing to be done. But he was wrong—and if you're going to say the same thing, you're wrong too. All Annie needs is rest." Mom wrung her hands together.

I knew if we'd stayed in Boise, Annie would have been able to go to her old doctor—would have been able to see him as soon as she needed to. Back in Boise, Annie had been doing better—so much so that Mom had decided it was safe for us to move. To get away from the trouble I'd gotten into. Mom thought Bolton would be a better place for all of us, a place to start over. Only Annie wasn't starting over. She was getting worse.

I stood behind my mother's chair, placing my hands on her shoulders. She patted my hand. Mom was always so sure that Annie would get better someday. And sometimes I let myself believe she would too. But deep down, I knew different. Deep down, I feared the worst. And deep down, I felt responsible.

"We could put her in the hospital, but there's not much else they can do for her." Doctor Goodman folded his arms and looked around the room as though he hoped he'd find an answer written on the wall. "I gave her a good dose of antibiotics," he said. Then, without Mom noticing, the doctor caught Sheriff Anderson's attention. He gave him the no-hope shake of his head, then picked up his medical bag. "Call me if there's any change, good or bad. Okay?"

"Of course," Mom said. Doctor Goodman reached for his heavy wool coat, and Mom added, "I can assure you, Doctor, it will be good news."

After the doctor left, I asked, "Should I sit with Annie? I mean, in case she needs something."

"Sure." Mom looked from me, then to the Sheriff. "Micah, why is Sheriff Anderson with you, and why are you out of school?"

"He wasn't feeling well." The sheriff stepped in. "So I brought him home. And please, call me Garth."

"You're sick?" She turned to me.

"I'm much better now, Mom." I wanted to wipe away the worried look on her face. "Probably something I ate." Not wanting to answer more questions, I headed for the living room but kept my ears tuned to my mother's voice.

"Since when does the school call the sheriff to deliver sick children home?" I heard Mom stirring the soup; the ladle scraped the tin bottom.

"You're forgetting this is a small town." That was the sheriff's deep voice. The soup stirring stopped. "Dawn, if I can do anything to help, I'd be more than happy to . . ."

A sob. A definite sob from Mom.

Then quiet.

Finally, I heard the cupboard door open, heard bowls being set on the countertop.

"Have you eaten lunch?" I heard Mom say. I bit at my thumbnail. She was asking him to eat with us.

"No. That looks mighty tasty." The sheriff sounded altogether too cheery.

"Have a seat."

"Only if I can bring supper to you tonight." More silence. I decided I'd had enough of eavesdropping and walked to Annie's bed.

She breathed deeply, sleeping hard.

Annie Bananie, you've got to get better. Mom and I need you.

I sat on the folding chair next to her bed and looked out the window at the intersection. I muttered, "I don't have till Christmas; I have to find whoever is building the Nativity now."

HAMMERHEAD

Annie slept through lunch. As soon as Sheriff Anderson left, my mother started a vigil at my little sister's bedside, softly stroking her hair from time to time and reading the Bible.

Not knowing what I could do to help, I cleaned the kitchen. When I was finished, I paced restlessly across the tile floor. I needed to return to the hardware store and question Mr. Jefferson. If I could find the baby Jesus and bring it back here before Annie woke up, I just knew it would somehow turn everything around.

I stood in the doorway leading into the living room and softly said, "Mom, is it all right with you if I go for a walk?"

"If you're sure you're feeling okay." She looked up from the Bible, bleary eyed. "I can't have you sick, too." Her face was pale. Dark half-moons hung beneath her eyes.

"I'm fine. I'll be back soon."

"I have to work tonight, but unless Annie's fever breaks, I'm staying right here." Mom gazed at Annie with a wary, watchful slant to her brows.

"I won't go far." I grabbed Dad's denim jacket and left.

As I neared Jefferson's store, I noticed a commotion going on in the front entryway. Wolfgang—the tramp—and Mr. Jefferson were arguing.

"I've told you before I don't want your kind hanging around my store. Now get your good-for-nothing hide out of here." Mr. Jefferson stood his ground. His warmed breath looked like puffs of steam. His hands were planted firmly on his hips.

"Don't mean nobody no harm." Wolfgang shook his head. "Just wanted to buy something. Don't stink, do I?"

"*Yes!* Now get out of here!" Mr. Jefferson slammed the door in the old man's face, nearly knocking him over.

"Money's money," Wolfgang mumbled as he walked past me. "Doesn't matter if you live in the dump; it buys the same."

I decided I could cross Mr. Jefferson off the list of people who might be building the Nativity. He sure didn't have the Christmas spirit.

I watched Wolfgang walk away, feeling bad for him. Then, suddenly, I had a thought. "Wolfgang!"

The old man stopped and looked up as if he'd heard a voice from above. Finally, he spied me, and a smile spread across his face.

"Ah, the gambler." His decayed, toothy grin spread from ear to ear. "I know you. Saw you playing your game in back of Miss Kora's."

I was tempted to set him straight, but right now it didn't matter whether or not he thought I'd been the one gambling. All that mattered was making him listen. "If you want, I'll go buy what you need if you give me the money." I crossed my fingers inside my jacket pocket, hoping he would take a chance.

Hesitantly, Wolfgang stroked his beard with his dirt-smudged hand. "I'm trusting, mind you, but I get the feeling you don't like me much. Why would you do this?"

Ashamed, I confessed my plan. "You give me your money, tell me what you want, and I'll go buy it for you . . . if you pay me three dollars and ninety-nine cents in return." I knew it was a lot of money for such a little chore, but I hoped Wolfgang would go for it.

The old man stared at me as if I were a creature from the dark side of the moon. After a long moment, he slowly turned away and fussed with his coat pocket.

The overcoat was so dirty and torn that I was amazed the ragged pocket held anything inside.

"It's a deal," Wolfgang said as he turned back to me. "Need a tarp. Got to protect my stash of pop bottles. Don't want nobody stealin' them."

I breathed a sigh of relief as he held out the money. Layers of dirt covered his fingers, which poked through threadbare gloves. His fingernails were jagged and filled with grit.

I hesitated only a moment, then reached out to receive the money.

The dollar bills Wolfgang laid in my hand were new and crisp. "That should be enough to buy the tarp. You bring it to me, and I'll pay you."

"A tarp," I repeated, inhaling cold air.

"Yep." The old man started to lumber off. "I'll wait behind Miss Kora's."

"No, in front of the Pharaoh Theater," I called out. I didn't want to meet him in the alley. What if he changed his mind and decided to beat me up instead of paying? Wolfgang seemed harmless, but I wasn't taking any chances.

"Makes no difference to me." Wolfgang shrugged. "Some people get a little antsy when I stand in front of their stores, but I pay them no mind." He ambled across the street, muttering to himself.

Once inside the store, I found a tarp right away. Mr. Jefferson looked over the purchase, then rung it up on the cash register. After paying him, I walked out as calmly as I could and then raced to the theater.

As I neared Wolfgang, I couldn't help noticing bank president Wellington walking past the old man. He covered his nose and gave Wolfgang a disapproving look, making sure there was plenty of space between them on the sidewalk.

Cautiously, I hid in the doorway of Kora's Kountry Kitchen and waited until Wellington had passed by. No need to draw attention to my dealings with the town tramp.

With the coast clear, I went over to Wolfgang. Handing him the tarp, I said, "Here you go."

"And here you go." Wolfgang handed me a buck fifty, turned, and walked away.

"Wait a minute. This isn't what you said you'd pay me!"

"Didn't tell you an amount—just said I'd pay you. 'Sides, it's all I have." The old man continued shuffling down the ice-splotched sidewalk.

"But . . ." This was not enough to buy the baby Jesus doll.

"Make the best of it." He winked, then turned the corner and disappeared behind the building.

Make the best of it!

I kicked at the snow and shoved the money into my pocket.

"What did that old drunk want?" The voice seemed to come out of nowhere.

Surprised, I jumped. I'd had no idea I was being watched. I turned around and saw Mr. Domingo speaking through the porthole of the ticket booth.

"I did him a favor." I tried to remain calm. "That's all."

"Well, you stay away from him. We don't need his kind around this town." Mr. Domingo slammed the porthole shut.

Squeezing the money in my hand, I glanced toward the hardware store, wondering if I could bargain with Mr. Jefferson, or at least ask him to hold the doll until I had more money. I had only taken a few steps toward the store when I heard someone call my name.

"Micah!"

Swinging around, I saw Horace and Ledge running down the sidewalk. They almost ran me over before stopping.

"I set up another craps game with Hammerhead Wilson," Ledge wheezed, trying to catch his breath.

Was he insane?

"See, I told Ledge you used to play," Horace sputtered.

I had confided in Horace, telling him the story of my troubles in Boise in hopes he would learn from my mistakes. I glared at him.

Horace grimaced and muttered, "Ledge told Hammerhead you played." He winced as if afraid I'd start yelling like his dad.

"The important thing is, you have a chance to win back what you lost covering for Horace," Ledge said. He seemed to want to make amends for what had happened last night.

The money Wolfgang had given me felt hot in my hand. My fingers itched. A game of craps could earn enough money to buy the doll. The baby Jesus could be Annie's. I might even win enough to buy something for Mom, too. Besides, the sheriff was already punishing me for playing; why not have the crime fit the punishment? "Where do we go?" I asked.

"Hammerhead's dad makes deliveries for Mr. Jefferson." Ledge squinted, looked up and down the street, and then softly said, "Anyways, Hammerhead wants to meet us in back of the hardware store. Didn't like playing behind the Kountry Kitchen."

"Is he good?" I couldn't take any chances.

"Nah." Ledge tugged at his stubborn coat sleeves, trying to cover the space of skin above his gloves. "Him winning last night was a fluke. Do you think a kid with a nickname like Hammerhead would be good at tossing dice?"

"Gosh, I mean," Horace gurgled with excitement, "he's as dumb as a post. He got his name 'cause when he's mad he butts you with his head. A couple of years back, he put a crack in Miss White's classroom door 'cause he missed Stinky Steiner."

"This sounds too good to be true," I muttered.

"Come on then." Ledge and Horace took off.

I hesitated. A dark feeling flickered over me, but I shook it off. "Wait up."

A BROKEN PROMISE

The delivery ramp to Jefferson's Hardware Store was protected by the cement stoop of the back door, which made it the perfect spot to play. Hammerhead's father kept the loading ramp free of snow, and from the top of the loading dock down the angular slope to the alleyway, the ramp was bare concrete.

Hammerhead Wilson rolled the dice back and forth between his plump, thick hands like he was trying to mold marbles out of the square dice.

All of my hopes and dreams for Annie rode on Hammerhead's toss. Over the course of the afternoon, I had increased my money to an incredible ten dollars.

Horace had assumed the role of cheering squad and hadn't actually played. Ledge had stayed in the game until the last throw. He'd lost five bucks and his gloves.

Now it was just between me and Hammerhead.

He looked up at me, the muscles in his thick neck rippling. "You a scaredy-cat, Connors? 'Fraid you might lose the money you've won?"

"Just drop the dice." I shifted my weight from one foot to the other.

Please, please roll snake eyes, I thought as I chewed on the end of my tongue. My kneecaps shook as if they were filled with jumping beans.

Finally, Hammerhead dropped the dice. The first die stopped. Two white spots shone. The other die rolled down the ramp. We followed it like squirrels chasing a nut. The die teetered then stopped. Five straight up.

"Unreal!" Hammerhead leaped for joy. He danced around. "Am I the best or what?"

I stared down at the five round dots. How could this have happened? The odds had been in my favor. How could I have lost all that money? The money to buy baby Jesus for Annie, the money to buy Mom's Christmas present, the money to bring life back to my family. Gone, all gone because of two little dice.

Then it dawned on me as if I'd just woken up. Hammerhead had cheated.

"You dirty, rotten cheater!" I lunged for Hammerhead's boulder body.

"What the—?" Hammerhead swatted me off like I was a pesky gnat.

"You cheated!" I leaped onto Hammerhead's broad back.

"Micah, he didn't cheat. Come on," Ledge said, wedging his arm between me and Hammerhead and trying to pry me off. Giving one last tug, Ledge broke my grip.

"He's gonna bunt you into the next county if you don't knock it off," said Ledge.

Hammerhead whirled around, his eyes ablaze. His quick mallet fist jabbed into my stomach.

Pain seared through me like an electric shock wave. It was all I could do to suck in air.

"Can you see?" Horace's freckled face was pinched with worry. "I mean, can you breathe?"

Hammerhead pulled back, taking aim again.

"Holy cow, let's get out of here!" Ledge grabbed hold of my coat's collar and started to run. Clutching my throbbing stomach, I barely kept pace with him. Horace took off in the other direction as if a fire-cracker had been lit in his pants.

Slipping and sliding, Ledge and I scrambled out onto Main Street's sidewalk. We turned to look down the alley. No sign of Hammerhead. The streetlights came on.

It was already dark.

How long had we been back there? I glanced up at the clock at the top of the courthouse. It bonged six times. Not only had I lost the money—I had completely lost track of the time. And what about Annie—was she all right? Mom would be sick with worry and late for work.

"You gonna be okay, Micah?" Ledge's hound-dog eyes studied me closely. "Your face is almost blue."

Ledge was full of surprises. Just when I thought I had the guy figured out, he up and did something nice, like save me from getting smashed by Hammerhead. But I was still leery; after all, he'd left me high and dry when the sheriff had caught us in back of the Kountry Kitchen. "I'm fine." I rubbed my stomach. "I better get home, though. Where's Horace?"

"I'll bet he's past the railroad tracks by now. Man, he doesn't get into fighting." Ledge yanked on his jacket sleeves in a futile effort to pull them over his blue-splotched wrists. Since he'd lost his gloves to Hammerhead, I knew his hands were bound to turn just as blue. "I better head home, too." He started to walk away, then turned and said, "Hey, I'll meet you tomorrow and we can find that baby Jesus, okay? This is gonna be the best Christmas joke this town has ever seen."

* * *

When I opened the door to the dimly lit stairway leading to my apartment, I saw my mother standing a few steps away. Even in this light, I could see that her eyes were firing darts. "You'd better have a broken leg," she said.

I'd never heard her voice take on such a furious tone.

"Is Annie okay?" My stomach still hurt from Hammerhead's punch, but I didn't say anything.

She turned away from me. "Her fever is down. Garth is sitting with her now."

Garth? It hadn't taken the sheriff long to weasel his way into our lives. Now Mom was relying on him when she should have been relying on me. I had failed in so many ways. Clenching my teeth, I fought the urge to justify my actions and instead softly said, "I'm sorry, Mom."

Stopping at the door, she turned. "Where have you been?"

I looked down at my wet canvas shoes. What could I say? No words came.

"You promised me you would be good in this town. You promised!" Her voice was shaky, the sternness gone now. I'd disappointed her again.

"I was worried about you." Mom studied my face, then sighed. "I've got to go to work. In the meantime, you're grounded." She shut the door hard as she left.

Knowing that Sheriff Anderson was sitting with Annie, I felt no desire to go inside and listen to yet another lecture.

But where else could I go? I was grounded. I stood there for a moment, mulling over my options. Then I remembered—there was one place I could go without disobeying Mom.

At the top of the stairs, I opened the storage closet. Climbing in over cardboard boxes and dodging broomsticks, I shut the door. It was pitch black in here, but I easily found my way through the darkness. I felt along the wall through the cobwebs to the plywood trapdoor in the ceiling. I had found this secret passage the day we'd moved into the apartment, when Mom had asked me to store the empty boxes in here.

Now I pulled myself up into the cold night air.

I'd often come here to think and to be by myself. I'd made a shelter out of a cardboard box and had lined the bottom with a few burlap potato sacks. The sacks smelled of dirt and spuds. I pulled one out and wrapped it around my hands like a muff. Stars shone like thousands of tiny mirrors in the moon's glow. But I had no intention of stargazing tonight.

Tonight I was determined to catch whoever was building the Nativity in the act.

Stepping lightly on the snowy rooftop, I walked to the walled edge. Leaning over, I could see the top of Annie's window, which faced the island intersection. This would be the perfect lookout. If anyone made a move to add something to the Nativity, I'd see them.

STOLEN MEAT

The courthouse clock chimed, reminding me that I been on the roof a very long time. I was freezing my feet off, and the burlap sacks were failing miserably at keeping my hands warm. Maybe this hadn't been such a good idea.

Pulling my arms out of my jacket sleeves, I hugged my body. My fists felt like snowballs, but I wasn't going to let cold hands stop me. I suppressed a shiver and concentrated on the street below.

President Wellington had just locked up the bank. Now he pulled his fur-lined coat collar around his drooping jowls and began walking down the street. How I wished Dad's jacket was fur-lined. Wellington hadn't gotten very far before he stopped and stared at something on the sidewalk. He looked in front of him and then behind, then reached down and picked up a coin. *Once a penny-pincher, always a penny-pincher,* I thought.

A few moments later, a brown delivery van that had "Jefferson's Hardware Store" blazoned on the side with bright red-and-yellow paint drove by. Hammerhead and his father. Even from the roof I could see the smug smile on Hammerhead's face. Who wouldn't be smiling with eleven dollars and fifty cents padding his pocket, along with Ledge's gloves?

Mr. Jefferson slowly ambled out of his building and locked the glass door. He tugged a knit stocking cap on his head and sluggishly made his way over to Gandy's Gas 'N Pump.

The minutes ticked by as the temperature continued to fall. Occasionally, the air brakes of diesels would squeal as the drivers geared down to travel through town, and a few people trudged in and out of Kora's Kountry Kitchen, but otherwise the street was silent and empty.

My entire body was numb. Overhead clouds swallowed the fading stars. "Please don't snow tonight," I mumbled. "I really don't want to shovel snow."

Just then I heard a truck stop in the alleyway in back of Kora's. Needing a change of scene, I stuffed my arms back into my coat sleeves and made my way to the rear of the building.

The delivery truck for Simpson Meats had arrived. Simpson's sold beef to the Kountry Kitchen. A tall, burly man with a face like Popeye's hefted several cases of packaged meat out of the truck and disappeared through the back entrance of the restaurant.

I was about to turn away when I heard something. Peering down, I saw Ledge. His movements were jerky, and he kept his eyes on the door of the building, all the while stuffing his jacket with packaged beef. No wonder he'd beat it out of there that night Sheriff Anderson had found us by the Kountry Kitchen. Not only had he been shooting craps—*he* was the one who had been stealing from Miss Kora!

"Ledge!" I shouted.

He looked up and saw me, and his eyes grew wide. Placing his index finger to his lips and making the universal sign for "be quiet," he began backing away from the truck.

I had to stop him. I hesitated for only a moment; it was tough enough to make friends in a new town without ratting on people. But as much as I didn't want to, I knew I had to tell the sheriff. It didn't matter that Ledge had saved me from Hammerhead. Covering for him playing dice was one thing, but covering for him stealing was quite another.

Bolting for the trap door, I crawled through the opening, dropped to the floor, and escaped from the closet. I flew down the stairs and burst out onto the street.

Ledge would be a long ways from the alley by now. Every morning he met up with Horace and me by the railroad tracks. He had to be heading that way.

Racing down the slick sidewalks, I came to the edge of town. I trudged up the small incline to the tracks. Walking down the rails was a tall, lean shape.

"Ledge, wait!" I raced to him.

"Who's watching your little sister?" Ledge kept his arms wrapped about his chest.

"Sheriff Anderson." I stumbled over the snow-covered railroad ties and jumped onto the iron rail of the tracks.

"Way to go, man." Ledge smiled and nodded at me. "Keep the law busy while I do my work."

"You've got to take the meat back!"

"Can't," Ledge said.

"Well, you *can't* just take it. It's not yours." I shivered and folded my arms tight, trying to hang on to some kind of warmth. "And what do you mean you *can't?* I don't see anyone twisting your arm."

"Come on, I'm freezing to death." Ledge kept trudging forward. "Don't want you tellin' anyone about this, okay?"

I slid off the rail and followed, still hopeful I could convince him to take the meat back. "But I have to."

Ledge stopped.

I collided into his back. "Sorry, but I have to tell. I'm already in trouble with Anderson."

"Look, I can't have the sheriff sniffing after me. My parents are gone." Ledge slid down the railroad bank. "See, Dad's a salesman, and he's on the road a lot. Mom goes with him. If the sheriff finds out I'm alone, he might take me away from my folks."

I slid down beside him, and Ledge continued.

"Mom and Dad get tied up with selling. Sometimes they don't get back for a week or so at a time. I don't mind being alone. Sometimes it's kinda cool. Man, I can sit up all night if I want."

"Don't you get scared, being alone?" I stepped over a bump in the snow.

Ledge headed for a small house guarded by thin, spiraling pines. The building looked dark and deserted.

"Nah. Got my dog, Ralph. He's a darn good watchdog." Ledge trudged up the wooden porch and kicked his boots against the door-post, knocking off clinging snow. He didn't look for his keys, just opened the door.

A dog started yapping, and Ledge flipped on the light.

I stepped inside and looked down on a fuzz ball of a dog. "This is Ralph, your guard dog?"

Ledge nodded.

"He looks like an electrocuted rat." The animal kept barking and yipping at me.

"Hey, knock it off." Ledge scowled at the dog.

Ralph ignored him. He stood in front of me, so focused on barking that with each *arf* his front legs lifted off the ground.

Ledge picked up a rolled newspaper and threw it at the animal.

Ralph yipped once more, then curled his tail between his legs and cowered into a corner where an old, tattered blanket lay.

I glanced around the room. A Franklin stove stood in the corner, and a well-worn couch sat on frayed carpeting in front of a television. I'd only ever seen TV sets in store windows. "So, why did you steal the meat?" I asked after a moment.

Ledge walked to the fridge. "Gotta eat. When Mom and Dad are here, they stock up, but like I said, sometimes they have a good run of sales and don't come back when they mean to." He pulled the meat packages from his coat and tossed them in the freezer.

I walked up behind Ledge and saw that the freezer was crammed full of top sirloin. "So you *are* the one who stole the two cases from Miss Kora's. You've got a whole freezer full! Why'd you steal more tonight?"

"It's Christmas." Ledge shut the fridge, then walked to the Franklin stove and crumpled some nearby newspapers, stuffing them inside the black mouth of the fireplace. "I wanted to surprise my folks with it." Ledge pulled kindling out of the woodbin and, once he had laid it on the paper, hefted a split log on top. "'Sides, Miss Kora has more food and money then she knows what to do with. She won't miss it none." Fishing a matchstick out of its container, he lit the fire.

"You shouldn't steal." I held my hands up to the flame. Heat. For the first time that night, I felt warmth. But I knew I couldn't think of myself right now. I somehow needed to convince Ledge to do the right thing. Jokingly, I said, "How are we going to find out who's building that Nativity if you get thrown in jail?"

"That won't happen if you don't snitch." Ledge tugged off his jacket, then turned on the TV. A test pattern came into focus. "Darn, I missed *Phil Silvers*. His show gets over at nine." He turned off the set and looked up at me. "You steal too."

"I do not!" I turned so my backside could get warm.

"What do you call playing dice? I mean, don't you feel like Hammerhead stole your money from you?" Ledge adjusted the antenna on the set, even though it was turned off.

"How can you say I was stealing? I lost, didn't I?"

Ledge shrugged. "That's the hitch with gambling—" he laughed, "—you might lose. My way, I always win." He ambled to the kitchen and opened the freezer door. Then he pulled out a neatly packaged sirloin steak and tossed it to me.

Automatically, my hands reached out and caught it.

"Take that to your mom. I know you need it. Shoot, you're poorer than I am." Ledge grabbed a can of root beer, then shut the fridge.

I stared at the package in my hands. *What if he's right? Is it okay to steal if you're poor—to take from people who have too much?*

I thought back on the doll I had almost stolen for Annie. It would have made her so happy, but something had stopped me—a feeling I couldn't describe. That same feeling smothered me now. I set the meat on the worn sofa cushion. "Are your folks going to be home for Christmas?"

"Oh, yeah. No sweat. They're probably doing some last minute shopping 'cause they're feelin' guilty for being gone so long. Last Christmas we got the television. They were gone for a month that time." Ledge tugged off his soggy, wet cowboy boots and plopped down on the couch.

"I'm glad they'll be home soon . . . I'd better go," I told Ledge. I didn't know why, but suddenly I knew I needed to leave. I felt confused, almost frightened.

"Hey, you forgot the meat." Ledge held up the package as I walked past him.

"No, that's okay. Be seeing you." I closed the door behind me and started running.

I ran until my sides burned, and sprinted up the stairs to my apartment. I slammed the door once I was inside.

I stood there, breathing hard. What had frightened me?

It hadn't been Ledge. And I wasn't scared of the night or of being out alone. I shook my head. I didn't know what had gotten into me, but I was glad to be home.

Wanting to check on Annie, even if it meant facing the sheriff, I stepped in the doorway to the living room.

Annie was sitting up in her bed, wide awake. She was working on the mini tinfoil shepherd staff. Shaping it into a crook at the top, she looked up and smiled.

Slumped in the folding chair next to her was the sheriff, his hat tipped over his face and his lanky legs stretched out.

"Hi, Micah," Annie said softly. "Did you see what's on the island?"

My heart dropped. *Please don't let anything new be there.* I walked to the window. The stoplight hanging over the stable reflected on two shepherds and three wise men.

"No!" I hit the wall.

"What . . ." The sheriff bolted from his chair. His hat rolled to the floor. He blinked a couple of times, then stared at me. "Young man, where have you been?"

LIFE SCARS

Sheriff Anderson's bloodshot eyes glared down at me. He ran one hand through his sleep-rumpled hair; the other hand rested on his hip above his holstered gun. The sheriff looked like a grumpy grizzly that had just come out of hibernation. I had to think fast.

"I was in the other room. Then Annie woke up, so I came in." I glanced at my sister.

She gave me an I-wish-I-could-help-you look. I winked at her.

"What were you doing in the other room all that time? You were awfully quiet." Sheriff Anderson picked up his hat.

"Reading . . . I was reading." I tried to sound casual.

"You were reading with the lights off?" The sheriff glanced at the darkened doorway between the kitchen and living room.

"Flashlight—Micah has a flashlight." Annie's small voice drew our attention.

Clearly surprised, Sheriff Anderson leaned against the wall. "I might not have believed Micah if he'd said that, but you, I believe." Annie's bottom lip drooped to a frown, and she sadly looked down at her crossed fingers.

"Truth is, Sheriff . . ." I glanced at Annie. I couldn't let her lie for me. ". . . I just got in."

The sheriff placed the brown folding chair in front of me. "Sit." I did as commanded.

"Now, where have you been, what have you been doing, and why have you been doing it? You were supposed to stay home." Sheriff Anderson didn't raise his voice or anything, but I expected an interrogation light to flash on at any moment.

Instead, the light in the kitchen came on, and Mom stepped into the room. Her eyes were filled with concern and outlined with black circles, yet she smiled.

"How's my Annie?" She ignored the sheriff and me and walked to my little sister's bedside.

"I'm much better, Mama. Look at the island. There are shepherds and wise men now." Annie pointed to the frost-coated window.

Mom looked out and smiled. She smoothed Annie's limp hair away from her forehead. "Your temperature is still down." She hugged Annie and then turned to the sheriff and me. "I'm surprised you're still here, Garth. I thought you'd leave when Micah came home at six."

"So did I." The sheriff raked his fingers through his straw-colored hair, then pulled on his hat. "Six, huh?"

I stared at the floor to avoid making eye contact with anyone. But sensing the sheriff's condemning look, I glanced up. "Yeah, six," I muttered, sure he was about to rat me out.

Sheriff Anderson pulled up the cuff of his uniform sleeve and checked his watch. Ledge had said that *Phil Silvers* got over at nine, so I knew it must be almost ten. The sheriff smiled with an I've-got-you-where-I-want-you expression on his face.

"Micah and I were getting on so well, time clean got away from us." I breathed a sigh of relief. He was playing it cool. "Been telling him about the new saddle I bought myself for Christmas. Why don't you let Micah come stay with me tonight? I'll see that he returns bright and early. You and Annie can have some time alone."

I furrowed my brow. Now what was the sheriff up to? No way would Mom let him take me home with him. She looked at the sheriff. There he stood—the symbol of law and order and all that was supposed to be right with the world. She had trusted him with Annie's care—and suddenly I knew she would trust him with mine as well.

"Is that what you want to do?" Mom gazed at me. She had a sixth sense when it came to people. That's why we'd rented from Miss Kora—because Mom had had a "feeling." From the look on her face, I knew she must be having the same kind of feeling now.

I wanted to go with the sheriff like I wanted a thousand bees stinging me. But with no way out, I answered, "Sure."

"Thanks, Garth," Mom said to the sheriff. She pulled off her black sweater and untied the white waitress apron. "Micah worries so about Annie and me. It'll be nice for him to have a break." She smiled at the sheriff like he had just performed a miracle.

How could I argue? For the first time in a long time, Mom looked relieved. I went to put on my jacket, resigned to my fate.

* * *

Once inside the patrol car, Sheriff Anderson turned to me. "Okay, Micah. What were you doing all those hours? You and the boys weren't playing another game, were you?"

"What game?" I asked, pretending to be puzzled.

The sheriff started the Fordor Sedan, and the heater whirred on. Checking the mirrors, he said, "What I can't figure out is where you'd play—it's freezing outside. Unless you went to Ledge's house. Were you with Ledge?"

"What?" I stared out the window.

"Were you with Ledge tonight?"

Now was my chance to tell the sheriff about Ledge stealing the meat. But I couldn't. I needed to give Ledge time to come to his senses and turn himself in. I was hopeful that with a little prodding from me, he would. So what could I say? I didn't want to tell the sheriff I'd spent most of the night on the roof trying to catch the Nativity builder. He already seemed suspicious of my interest in whoever was building the Nativity, and I didn't want him watching me any more closely than he already was. If he so much as thought I'd done something wrong, he'd have me shoveling all of Main Street until spring.

"Come on." The sheriff stopped the car in front of Jefferson's.

"Where are we going?"

"I have to do my rounds, and you're coming with me. Maybe a little work will loosen your tongue." When the sheriff opened the car door, a wave of frigid air swished in.

Bracing myself against the cold, I grudgingly followed as the sheriff checked the locks at the hardware store, the bank, the courthouse, Doc Goodman's, and all the small stores that lined Bolton's Main Street. Neither one of us said a word as we walked.

When we were finished, Sheriff Anderson and I climbed back into the patrol car. As he started down the road, I wondered out loud, "Where do you live?"

"Got a place out by the Larken family. They tend to keep to themselves pretty much. Weeks will go by, and all I'll see is Ledge walking to school. I know his father travels a lot." The sheriff quit talking, as if waiting for me to spill my guts and say something that would get Ledge in trouble.

I tried to ignore him. When he drove past Ledge's house, I saw that a light was still on. Did the sheriff suspect that Ledge was alone? If he did, why didn't he do something? Wasn't there a law against kids living alone? I decided that while Sheriff Anderson might suspect something, he didn't know for sure.

"What do you think?" asked the sheriff.

"What do I think?" I repeated, not sure what he was talking about.

"Yeah, what do you think?" Sheriff Anderson turned into a driveway, which led to a small brick house. In the carport was a two-door, hardtop Studebaker, a car much like the one my father had always wanted and the one I'd dodged the other day.

"Someone staying with you?" I asked, hoping to sidetrack him.

The sheriff's gaze followed mine. "No, that's my car. I don't drive it very often. Just take it for a spin every once in a while. Drove it over to Miss Kora's the other day. In fact, that was the day I met you." He put the patrol car in park and turned to look at me. "Now, what should we do about you not coming home when your mother thought you did and not fessing up to where you've been all evening?"

"I don't know." Wanting to escape, I opened my door and got out.

"I've been wondering," the sheriff began as he got out of the car and pulled house keys from his uniform jacket pocket. "How does it feel to watch your little sister lie for you?" He waited for a reply. I couldn't tell him the truth—that it felt worse than when Hammerhead had sucker punched me in the stomach. After a few moments, the sheriff said, "I want to help your family, but I get the feeling you're not so keen on that idea." Then he walked up the steps and opened his front door.

"We don't want or need your help," I said. The sheriff stepped inside and turned on the overhead light.

As I walked inside and closed the door, I noticed that in the middle of the living room was a new leather saddle on a sawhorse. He really did have one. I gazed about the room. An old, tan recliner sat in front of a big radio. Books were stacked all over—on the floor, on the coffee table, beside the chair, and in the windowsills.

"Let me take your coat." The sheriff hooked his hat on the saddle's horn.

I craned my head, trying to read the titles of some of the books as I slipped off my jacket: *The Adventures of Sherlock Holmes, Weapons,* and *Criminology.*

"I like to read. Takes up the time." Sheriff Anderson hung my dad's jacket in the closet and placed his coat next to it. "Your coat is a bit big for you. Was it your father's?"

"Maybe."

"Doesn't look like it keeps you very warm."

"Works for me."

"Okay. So, when you were out doing whatever you were doing, did you eat?"

I hadn't eaten since lunch, ten hours ago. But standing there, twining my fingers together, I said nothing.

"Does everything have to be a struggle with you?" Sheriff Anderson yawned and rubbed his chin. "Well, whether you're hungry or not, I am. If you want something, follow me."

In the kitchen, my eyes focused on the cupboards. I hadn't seen such beautiful wood since Dad made Mom's rocker. My father had loved making things with his hands, and I had loved watching him as he gently crafted the wood into furniture. Dad had done his projects in the basement of our Boise apartment building. The landlord hadn't minded. So Dad had been able to build Mom's rocker without her knowing. I'd tried to help but had only managed to drop a chisel on Dad's hand, cutting him. That day seemed a million years ago. My gaze returned to the cupboards. "What kind of wood is this?"

Sheriff Anderson rummaged in the freezer. "It's knotty pine. Made those myself."

If the sheriff knew how to make cabinets like this, he was mighty handy with a saw. The fact that he did something other than enforce the law surprised me. But then I had never really thought about what police officers did at home. I thought on this some more. I knew the sheriff liked horses; the saddle in his living room gave that away. He liked cars; the Studebaker in the carport told me that. And it seemed he was also a part-time carpenter. He was so like Dad . . . yet so different.

"Supposed to be a big storm tonight." The sheriff shut the freezer and moved on to the fridge. "You'll need something hearty to give you 'shovel strength' in the morning."

Out of the blue, a thought hit me. "It's you. I should have known. You're the one building the Nativity."

"No." He pulled a casserole from the refrigerator and set it on the counter. "Wish I'd have thought of it though. Why is it so important for you to figure out who the Nativity builder is?"

"Just curious." I'd thought for sure Sheriff Anderson was the one.

"It's more than curiosity. You can trust me, Micah. I've been watching you the last couple of days. You're not like the others."

"What do you mean, I'm not like the others?"

He placed the casserole in the oven and then turned his full attention on me. "I know Ledge will end up in trouble with the law most of his life. I know Horace is a follower. But you—you're different. You have what I call 'life scars.' Your mom told me your father died in Korea."

I nodded, wondering what my father had to do with any of this and what business it was of the sheriff's.

Sheriff Anderson continued. "She told me that you've been the man of the house since your father's death. I just wanted you to know that if you need help, I'm here." He smiled and patted my shoulder.

I pulled back slightly and looked away. Sheriff Garth Anderson may have wormed his way into my mother's heart, but he wasn't going to get to me. "We're fine. I'm fine, Mom's fine, and Annie will be *fine*. Just wait and see. As soon as I can get my hands on that stupid baby . . ."

Too late, I realized I'd said too much. "We'll be fine!" I said, flustered. I wasn't going to discuss this anymore. "Where do I sleep?"

HOPPING MAD

December 24, 1953

I slept in the sheriff's flannel-lined sleeping bag. It felt so good to be warm, and the plush lining made it feel like I was drifting on clouds. But all too soon, Sheriff Anderson was standing above me, telling me it was time to get up. Snow had fallen in the night.

The sheriff fed me homemade waffles swimming in maple syrup. This struck me as odd, since he'd said he ate at the Kountry Kitchen every morning. *Maybe he just goes there for the company,* I thought.

Breakfast was over much too quickly, and then we were off. Pulling up to the curb in front of the theater and the restaurant, Sheriff Anderson said, "Wait a minute. I can't stand to watch you shovel snow with only those tennis shoes on your feet." He reached over the seat and grabbed a pair of boots. "I wore these when I was a boy. My mother kept everything."

I studied the boots. "These are brand new." No way had these boots belonged to the sheriff when he was a boy.

"Really?" Sheriff Anderson smiled. "I thought they were my old ones. Anyway, they don't fit me; you might as well wear them."

Although it was obvious he was making this up, I decided to accept the boots anyway. I didn't like having cold toes any more than the next guy. As I jammed my feet into the rubber boots, I felt the sheriff's eyes on me. So maybe it made him feel good to help a poor kid. What harm was there in that? I quickly fastened the clasps.

"Take this too." The sheriff handed me a new jacket with a fur collar and a fancy zipper.

I looked from the coat to the sheriff, suspicious now. "I think I know why you're doing this. See, I've been wondering why you didn't keep grilling me last night when I was late coming home. You even covered for me with Mom, then brought me home with you and fed me." I shoved the warm jacket away. "All that talk about me being different from the other guys was baloney, wasn't it? What you're really thinking is that I'm the problem between you and my mom. And you think by giving me a coat I'll forget my dad and decide I like you. Well, I don't need your coat."

Flustered and angry, I jerked off the boots. "And I don't want your boots. Where's the stupid shovel?"

"You're wrong," Sheriff Anderson said quietly and shook his head. "I was just trying to do you a favor. Can't you see the snow?"

"Got eyes, don't I?" I glared at him.

"You may have eyes, but it's your brain I'm worried about. Common sense would tell you to wear boots and a warm coat to shovel snow." With that, the sheriff jerked open his car door and made his way to the rear of the vehicle.

I followed. Sheriff Anderson unlocked the trunk, pulled out the snow shovel, and slammed the trunk shut. "Kid, you're wrong about me."

"Well, you're wrong about me, too," I replied.

As I turned away, I caught a glimpse of the island intersection.

Two new figures were there.

The snow shovel slipped from my hands. Kicking through the snow, I ran to the Nativity.

In the protection of the stable knelt a beautiful Mary, and standing beside her was Joseph. They were carved out of wood and had been painted with fine detail. Joseph held a lantern in his right hand as he leaned over his wife. Mary's arms were folded in her lap. There was a peaceful, contented look on her face as she gazed at the manger where the baby Jesus would soon lay.

"Who's doing this?" I clenched my hands into fists and crossed my arms tightly over my chest.

"It's all right." The sheriff patted my shoulders.

I was in no mood to be comforted. In fact, I was hopping mad. "You know, don't you?" I accused through clenched teeth. Sheriff

Anderson grasped my arms, knelt beside me, and said, "I honestly don't know who's doing this. Why is it upsetting you? Look . . ." He glanced over his shoulder. "Aren't they beautiful? Someone's trying to do something wonderful for the whole town. It's a present. And for the life of me, I can't figure out why you're so upset."

A chill swallowed me, and I tugged away from the sheriff. "No. All you care about is whether the sidewalks are shoveled and whether there's anyone having fun so you can punish them." I paused for a moment. "And you're wondering how long it will take to steal my mother and my sister away from me."

I turned and walked back to the shovel, picked it up, and started working on the sidewalks.

Sheriff Anderson stood stone still by the Nativity figures for a long moment. Then he slowly made his way to the car.

RATTING

I worked as hard and fast as I could. The snow was heavy and wet and clung to the shovel blade with each scoop. My feet were soaking, and my hands were so cold that I could barely feel them, but I kept working.

When I finished, I didn't bother to say anything to Sheriff Anderson, who had been keeping an eagle eye on my every move from the patrol car. I leaned the shovel against the black-and-white sedan and sprinted for the door to the stairs of my apartment without looking back.

I leapt up the steps two at a time and reached for the doorknob just as the door opened. Doctor Goodman stood in front of me. Deep, furrowed lines were wedged between his bushy, white eyebrows. His face was tinted with gray shadows, and his shoulders were slumped. He looked like he'd just lost a fight. The creases on his face softened when he realized who I was. "Hi, son. I understand you stayed with the sheriff last night."

I hated when adults I didn't really know called me "son." But mostly, I hated the tone in the doctor's voice—too sweet and too full of pity. "Is Annie all right? What happened? Her fever was down."

"What's going on, Doc?" Sheriff Anderson stood behind me.

Doctor Goodman didn't answer either one of us right away. He finished buttoning his black winter coat and then said, "About 4:30 this morning, Mrs. Connors called me. The little girl's fever had spiked again. I guess she's had so much of these antibiotics that they don't work for long anymore. 'Bout all we can do now is keep her comfortable. Sure wish I could give the child more time. She's such a sweet little thing."

I pushed past the doctor and raced to the living room. Mom was on the bed next to Annie. They were both asleep, with Mom's arm wrapped protectively around my little sister.

Annie looked like she always had. And despite the fact that her cheeks were flushed and her lips a pinkish purple, she still looked like an angel to me.

I could tell my mother had been crying; her eyelids were puffy, and her swollen cheeks were red as if they'd been sunburned. Her hair, which was usually fastened in a bun or a braid, hung loose and draped down over her arms and back. She wore her old, tattered bathrobe, the one my dad had given her so long ago. Once a bright red, it was now a faded rose color with holes in the thready pockets.

"Should we fix them some breakfast?"

I jumped and turned to find Sheriff Anderson standing behind me. "What?" How could he be thinking about food right now?

The sheriff nodded toward the kitchen as if he didn't want to disturb Mom or Annie with our talking.

Once we were in the kitchen, he said, "Doc told me your mom's been up since three this morning. She hoped the fever would go down on its own but finally had to call the doctor. Doc said he's been sitting there watching the two of them sleep for a couple of hours." The sheriff opened the cupboard door. "What does your mom like for breakfast?"

There were a few cans of tomato soup, a sack of bread with only the dried heels left, and the neatly wrapped spice cookies from yesterday.

"*I'll* make my mother's breakfast," I told him and folded my arms.

"Well, you can't make anything for breakfast until you have something to make it with." The sheriff nudged his cowboy hat to the back of his head. "I'll run down to Gandy's and see what I can find. In the meantime, you'd better get those wet shoes off before you catch your death." The word *death* hung in the air as if it would suck the life from the room.

A knock sounded at the door.

"You expecting somebody?" asked the sheriff as he opened it.

"Whoa." Ledge's eyes grew wide as he focused on Sheriff Anderson. "Man, what happened here?"

"Mr. Larken." The sheriff smiled and tugged his hat straight. "You're up pretty early for a Saturday morning. Do your folks know where you are? Or better yet, do you know where your folks are?" The sheriff tapped his fingers on the wooden door.

Glaring at me, Ledge spat out, "You little ratfink. Just because you took the fall for the craps game didn't mean you had to go ratting to the sheriff about my parents. Besides, the game was really Hammerhead's idea. And I came here to help you!" He scowled. "You told him about the meat too, didn't you? I thought you were my friend!"

I shook my head vigorously, trying to shut Ledge up, but it was too late.

"Man, don't shake your head at me." Then Ledge saw the sheriff's expression. He stopped talking, and his eyebrows peaked like question marks. When understanding dawned on him, his head drooped and his shoulders hunched. He looked from the sheriff to me. "I just blew it, didn't I?"

Forcing a weak smile, I slowly nodded.

"So Hammerhead participated in the game as well," Sheriff Anderson said, slowly shaking his head. "I'll give his folks a call after I take care of you. Ledge, do you have any relatives—aunts or uncles—who live close by?" The sheriff folded his arms.

"Got an uncle up by Table Rock." Ledge swiped a hand over his face.

"Good." Sheriff Anderson patted Ledge's shoulder. "That's about a two-hour drive from here. I'll give your uncle a call. You shouldn't be alone on Christmas Eve. In the meantime, I believe you said something about meat—top sirloin perhaps?" The sheriff sucked air between his teeth, then looked from me to Ledge.

Ledge swallowed so hard I could hear him gulp.

"That's what I thought. Looks like the rest of Main Street will get shoveled today. When you're finished, we'll have a talk with Miss Kora. Come on." He pulled Ledge toward the stairs. "Micah, tell your mom I'll come by sometime tonight."

I followed them out of the apartment and stood at the head of the stairs, watching the sheriff take Ledge away. I felt bad for him, but I also knew the sheriff was doing what had to be done.

However, now I'd have to find the baby Jesus by myself.

THE BLUE SPRUCE

Staring down on the Nativity, I racked my brain, trying to figure out who could be building the scene. I was plain out of hunches and didn't know what to do next. I wondered if it might just be best to wait until late that night when the baby Jesus was dropped off and then borrow it for Annie. She just had to hang on until then.

I looked over at Gandy's Gas 'N Pump and saw a family buying a Christmas tree. I glanced around the apartment. It felt so bare and cold, like it was just waiting for Annie to give up. What she needed was something to live for—a Christmas Eve that was filled with holiday cheer. Wouldn't Mom and Annie be surprised if when they woke up I had a Christmas tree waiting for them?

But trees cost money.

I had priced the beautiful blue spruce I'd seen at Gandy's Gas 'N Pump. Mr. Gandy wanted two dollars a foot for it, and he wanted a dollar a foot for the other scraggly trees.

Where else could I get a tree besides Gandy's? Bolton was in the middle of a desert. No pine trees here, just plenty of sagebrush on the outskirts of town.

Sagebrush! Some of those bushes were taller than me. I grinned. Maybe we'd have a Christmas tree after all this year.

I glanced at my mother and Annie again. They were sleeping soundly, and I knew they probably wouldn't wake up for hours. I could risk a quick trip to find a sagebrush for our Christmas tree.

The floor creaked as I tiptoed out of the room. As I grabbed Dad's jacket off my cot, I decided I'd better leave a note, just in case Mom woke up and got worried about me.

I spotted a brown paper sack we used for garbage. I tore off a piece and dug through the junk drawer until I found a broken navy-blue crayon. After scribbling a note that simply said, "Be back soon. Love, Micah," I leaned the note against the cup holding the pink, plastic tulip on the dining table. As I was about to walk out the door, I realized I had nothing to cut down the sagebrush with. I certainly couldn't break a sagebrush trunk with my bare hands. I needed something sharp.

I opened the silverware drawer, looking for something with jagged edges that I could use as a saw. Aha! I pulled out a long bread knife. This would work fine. However, I couldn't very well walk down the street holding the knife for all to see, so I slipped it up my coat sleeve. Armed and ready, I left.

Once out of town, I sunk knee-deep in the snow-blanketed fields. My canvas shoes quickly soaked through, but I refused to think about cold toes.

Where are all the tall ones? I thought as I scanned the field. Most of the bushes were covered by tiny mounds of snow, but I finally spied a larger bush poking out of the snowdrifts across the way on the south bank of the Burgen Canal.

Trudging up to the bank, I could see that the canal was dry except for a few frozen puddles, protected from the snow by cottonwood trees and the canal banks. Some of the icy patches looked big enough to ice-skate on.

Wouldn't Annie enjoy ice-skating? I mused. Then, before I could stop it, a thought flashed through my mind: *She never will.*

No! I shook my head and quickly busied myself with the sagebrush. This one would do nicely. Kneeling, I cleared the snow away from the trunk and began sawing.

* * *

It took all morning and part of the afternoon to saw down the ornery sagebrush. Twice the knife stuck and jammed the blade into a kink. When I finally finished, I knew I'd have to hurry home.

Dragging the bush by the trunk, I made it back to town. But as I passed Gandy's Gas 'N Pump, I realized I didn't have a tree stand.

I looked over the remaining pine trees that were lined up in front of the store and saw that the blue spruce was still there in all its glory. Shrugging, I bent down to see two slabs of wood crisscrossed and nailed onto the tree's trunk. So that's how it stood.

"Gotcha a tree there, huh?"

I jumped up to see Mr. Gandy standing in the doorway of his store. He stroked his white beard, eyeing my sagebrush.

Scratching his balding head, Gandy walked around the bush. "Never would've believed it. Pretty tree for sagebrush. What kind of stand do you have?"

I cleared my throat. "Thought I'd do kinda what you did here." I nodded at the blue spruce.

"Well," Mr. Gandy pulled at his green and red suspenders, "why don't we slap one of those thingamajigs on the trunk of your Christmas bush?"

He disappeared into the store and returned with a hammer and nails in hand. Then Mr. Gandy snaked out a couple of loose wooden slabs from under the trees and, quick as the Flash, nailed the boards to my sagebrush and stood it upright.

I slapped my fist into my hand excitedly. Then, as quickly as my joy had risen, it fell. "I don't have any money to pay you. I should have said something before."

Mr. Gandy winked. "Merry Christmas . . . Micah, is it?"

I nodded. "Micah Connors."

"Merry Christmas, Micah Connors." Then Mr. Gandy stepped back into his store.

* * *

"What in the world?" Mom stood at the stove stirring a pot, still dressed in her old tattered bathrobe, as I stumbled into the apartment dragging the bush.

"Do you like it?" I placed the bush in the middle of the kitchen then stepped back, proud of my accomplishment.

"I've never seen anything like it." Her hands to her cheeks, Mom circled the sagebrush. She stopped and wiped away a tear. "What a beautiful tree."

"How's Annie?" I asked and tugged off my jacket.

"Still sleeping," Mom said, and quickly moved to stir the pot, which had started bubbling.

I wrapped the bread knife in my jacket and laid it on my bed. I didn't want my mom to know I'd used her bread knife—especially since the blade was now bent in two places.

Mom tapped the spoon on the side of the pot and gestured toward the bush. "You know, that's not your ordinary, everyday kind of Christmas tree. It has character, a charisma all its own."

I smiled, but a dull pain throbbed in my chest. I knew she longed for the years of perfect Christmases as much as I did—the years before Dad died. But Mom would never let on to me. Last year we hadn't even had a tree. Mom had been working as a janitor at the hospital in Boise. She'd had to work all Christmas Day. Annie and I had made garland chains out of old newspapers to hang over the doorways. That had been our Christmas.

"Micah, there's some boxes out in the storage closet. I think there's some old tree lights in one of them." As she pulled the pot off the stove, a knock came at the door.

I opened it to find Miss Kora. She bustled in wearing jingle bell earrings, a red sequined shirt, and dark red pants. She held a couple of grocery bags. "Where can I put these, kid?"

"Huh?" I didn't know what to say.

"Oh, my stars!" My mother dropped her wooden stirring spoon, her hands shaking. "I can't believe your generosity."

"What's not to believe? You never heard of a Christmas bonus?" Miss Kora began unpacking the groceries. "Here, kid, put this in the fridge." She handed me a turkey—the biggest one I'd ever seen. I set it on the bottom rack and turned to close the door just as Miss Kora handed me a carton of milk and a carton of eggnog, a dozen eggs, carrots, potatoes, celery, frozen orange juice, a bag of oranges and apples, and whipping cream. Our fridge hadn't been this full in years.

"Let's put these rolls and that bread up in the cupboard." Miss Kora popped her gum as she placed the goods on the wooden shelf. She peered into the brown sack again. "There's still some packages of Jell-O, Kool-aid, and a bag of candy left to be put away. I need to run downstairs. I've got a pot of clam chowder on the stove with bread-sticks in the oven."

My stomach growled. Mom looked at the leftover soup in the pot.

Miss Kora followed her gaze. "Don't tell me you're eating already." She glanced at her gold wristwatch. "It's only four thirty."

"Bad night and day," my mother told her.

"Hmm . . ." Miss Kora glanced at the soup pot again, hesitated a moment, and then said to me, "Kid, you ever hear of a potluck dinner?"

I shook my head.

"That's when everybody puts their dinners together. So I'm going to go ahead and get the chowder." She stopped in front of the sage-brush.

"What in the name of Halley's comet is this?" Miss Kora clicked her tongue.

"It's our Christmas tree." Mom smiled. She brushed her loose hair over her shoulder, then glanced down at her holey bathrobe and pulled it more snugly around her.

"I was afraid you were going to say that." Folding her arms, Miss Kora circled the tree. "You know . . ." She paused, studying the bush. "It grows on you. Yeah, it'll do." Then her eyes lit up like the Fourth of July. "In fact, I've got some of that spraying snow—you know, the kind in the can?"

My mother nodded, like she thought this was a brilliant idea.

Then Miss Kora's painted eyebrows arched high over her blue eyes. "We could even put glitter on the tree. Got lots of that. I use it once in a while in my hair. Adds emphasis, you know. I'll be right back," she called as she hurried out the door.

"Quick, Micah, go and get our tree lights before she comes back." Mom scurried toward her bedroom. "I need to change."

Brimming with excitement, I hurried to the closet and dug through the boxes. Pulling out the crumpled paper garland from last year, I found the multicolored Christmas tree lights.

When I returned to the apartment, I placed the garland on the dining table and got to work draping the tree lights on the bush. Just as I finished, Miss Kora returned.

She set the chowder on the stove and placed the breadsticks in a wicker basket she'd brought along. Then, reaching into a grocery sack, she pulled out two cans of snow spray. "This is gonna be fun, kid. You take one, and I'll take one."

She shook her snow can, so I shook mine, and then we started spraying, careful to avoid getting snow on the lights. It wasn't long before it looked like a snow cloud had blitzed the bush.

Miss Kora reached back into the sack and pulled out a bottle of gold glitter. "This is going to get all over, you know. And if I wasn't the landlady, I'd say don't tell her." She winked.

I put the empty snow spray cans in the garbage while Miss Kora sprinkled the gold dust over the bush. Once this task was complete, she handed me the glitter bottle. "You know, I'd love to stick around for the rest of the festivities, but I've got a hot date."

"But what about the potluck?" I asked, unable to hide the disappointment in my voice. I didn't want her to leave. She filled the room and made it feel like Christmas.

"You go ahead without me—I might sneak back. Sometimes these dates don't work out. Later, kid." She winked, popped her gum, and left before I could say anything else.

I decided to take the tree into Annie's room. She had to be awake—I'd seen Mom sneak into the living room while Miss Kora was sprinkling glitter. Boy, would Annie be excited to see this.

Mom was sitting beside Annie, holding her hand. She was dressed in her flowered duster, and her silky hair still hung loose and was draped like a shawl over her shoulders.

Annie's eyes were open, but she wasn't sitting up. She looked so sick. Her cheeks were red, and her hair was damp from the fever. My little sister stared at the bush as I slid it into the room.

"Hey, Annie Bananie." I tried to be cheery. "Thought you were going to sleep for two days. Got us a tree. We need your expert advice on where to put it."

"It's beautiful, Micah." Annie slightly smiled and licked her chapped lips. But she didn't raise a hand to show me where to put the tree.

"How about I set it over here, where the plug-in is?" I hefted Mom's rocker out of the corner, then pushed the bush in place. I belly-crawled under the bush and said, "Okay, Mom, turn out the lights."

I heard her walk to the switch. When the room turned dark, I plugged in the tree lights, then crawled out and backed away, excited to see what the bush looked like. The lights twinkled brightly, their beams reflecting off the golden glitter on the lacy, white branches.

Not bad. Not bad at all.

I glanced at Annie. She couldn't see the bush as well as I'd hoped from where she lay. I dashed around to the other side of her bed and helped her ease onto her side.

As her big brown eyes focused on the brilliant scene, she gasped and whispered, "It looks like an angel tree."

And that's what it looked like to me, too, especially as I stood there holding my little sister. "Miss Kora and I sprayed it with canned snow and sprinkled glitter over it. You're right, it is an angel tree."

"The shepherd staff. Where is it?" Annie asked softly. I searched over the bed, then looked on the card table. The shepherd staff lay next to the medicine bottles.

"I want to put it on the tree." She tried to get up but collapsed back onto her pillows. I handed her the tinfoil staff.

"I'll tilt the bush toward her," Mom said. "Micah, you help her with the staff." Mom went to the bush, and I eased Annie onto her side again. She raised her hand halfway and stopped. Just this brief motion had drained her of her energy. I took hold of her hand and guided it to the bush. She hooked the tiny, silvery shepherd's staff on the snowy branch. Annie's tear-pooled eyes reflected the Christmas tree lights as I eased her back onto the pillows.

"Thanks," Annie whispered, continuing to look in the direction of the tree. "I wish I could see it all the time." She licked her lips.

I didn't know what to do. I couldn't move the bush. It had to stay by the electrical outlet.

"I know, Annie," Mom said. Dabbing her eyes, she quickly tucked her hanky in her dress pocket. "We'll roll up a towel and nestle it up to your back, so you'll have support. And by tomorrow, you'll have your strength back and be sitting on your own. I'll go get the towel right now." She rushed out of the room.

Someone knocked on the door. It had to be Miss Kora. She'd said she'd come back if things didn't work out on her date. "I'll get it," I said and sprinted past my mother. I was anxious for Miss Kora to see the bush now with the Christmas lights turned on.

When I opened the door, all I could see were evergreen boughs.

"Ho, ho, ho! Merry Christmas!" In stepped Sheriff Anderson with the blue spruce Christmas tree.

THE ANGEL TREE

I fumbled with the doorknob. What could I do? What could I say? I looked at the perfect, proud blue spruce and knew the answer. Nothing. Annie deserved the best Christmas possible.

"Like the tree?" The sheriff grinned, standing the spruce in the center of the kitchen. "Even bought some ornaments for it. Set them outside the door there. Want to grab them?" Sheriff Anderson took off his coat and crossed the room, his cowboy boots crushing the sprinkles of glitter that had fallen from the angel tree. He laid his jacket on the table, pushing aside our homemade garland from last year.

I glanced out the doorway. On the entry mat was a cardboard box full of shiny new balls, stars, and holly wreaths. Grabbing the ornaments, I shut the door and set the box on the counter. "Who is it, Micah?" Mom walked into the kitchen, the rolled towel in her hands. Her whole face lit up like summer sunshine when she saw the tree.

"Oh, my stars!" She squeezed the towel until her knuckles were white. Then her gaze rested on me, and a look of concern tugged at the corners of her eyes. She smiled, then turned back to the sheriff and said, "It's a lovely tree, Garth, but we already have—"

"Mom," I broke in. "I know the perfect place for this." Tapping her arm to let her know I would take care of everything, I said, "I'll be right back."

Turning so my mom couldn't see, I grabbed the scratchy blanket off the cot I slept on.

* * *

Annie was asleep when I walked into the living room. I tried to tiptoe past her.

"Micah, I love our angel tree." Her voice was a mere whisper.

I did my best to make my voice upbeat. "Me too, Annie. But, well, I still need to do some work on it. It's not quite finished." I unplugged the lights and threw the blanket over the bush. "I'm gonna take it back into the kitchen. The sheriff brought a tree to fill in while I fix this one." Hefting the covered bush in my arms, I glanced back at Annie. A puzzled look creased her face. As I approached the archway, Sheriff Anderson lugged the perfect tree into the room and sat it in the vacated corner.

Pine scent filled the air. The bluish green branches of the tree reached regally upward, proud to be a Christmas tree.

I glanced at Annie again. She was still staring at me with that puzzled expression.

"Isn't it beautiful?" Mom took Annie's hand.

Annie still didn't take her eyes off me.

"Annie Bananie." I couldn't just walk away. Setting the bush down, I pointed to the spruce and said, "That's the most beautiful Christmas tree we've ever had." I smiled at her and walked to her side. "At least look at it."

"Do you promise to bring the bush back? I want the baby Jesus to see our angel tree and the shepherd staff." There was determination in Annie's tired eyes.

"Why don't we put the shepherd staff on this tree?" I said. Sheriff Anderson set his hat on the card table beside the bed and glanced toward the blanketed lump by the archway.

"But the baby Jesus should see the angel tree first." Annie coughed. Sweat beaded across her forehead.

"Is that what you have under that blanket? A tree?" The sheriff started toward the bush, but Mom pulled him back.

"Micah is still working on his tree." She gazed at me, and I knew she understood. I didn't want the sheriff to see my little bush next to his impressive tree.

"Annie, I told you I'd fix it and bring it back. Now please look at that tree." I pointed to the corner.

Annie glanced in the direction of the spruce without turning her head. "It is beautiful." She smiled at the sheriff.

"Well, let's decorate it." Sheriff Anderson went to the kitchen and returned with the ornaments. I slid my tree out of the living room and began pushing it toward the door.

Mom walked into the kitchen before I could take the tree out. "Where are you going?"

I was too upset to answer. Biting my tongue, I walked to my bed and hurriedly grabbed my jacket. The bread knife dropped to the floor at my feet.

Mom looked at the knife, then at me. "I was wondering how you cut down the bush."

"I'm sorry, Mom. All that work, I bent your good bread knife, and for what?" I picked up the blade.

"Annie loves your tree." Mom said softly and went to the cupboard for the soup bowls.

"I know, but now she can have the best. Maybe after Christmas we can put the angel tree back up." I tossed the knife in the garbage sack and slipped on my jacket.

"Where will you put your tree until then?" Mom pulled soupspoons out of the drawer.

"I'll stick it in the outside storage closet." I opened the door and picked up the bush. The light cord dangled to the floor.

"Hurry back. It's Christmas Eve, and I want us together tonight. It's important, Micah." A serious expression framed her face and clouded her eyes.

I looked up at Mom and nodded. But the Christmas cheer I'd felt earlier was gone. Why was this happening? And why did Annie have to be the sick one anyway? I knew it should be me. After all, I was the one who was always getting into trouble.

"Don't let Garth's tree ruin our evening. He's just trying to help us," Mom said. She gave me a hug, then dipped the soup ladle into the chowder.

"I know," I replied with a sigh, opening the door. "Will you shut this behind me? I've got my hands full." I wrestled the bush out, and Mom set the ladle down.

"Hurry back," she said before closing the door.

As I slid the bush into the storage room closet, I glanced up at the roof. Maybe if I had some fresh air I would feel better so I could go back inside and enjoy Christmas Eve with Mom and Annie . . . and the sheriff.

I scrambled onto the rooftop. For a moment, standing on the snow-covered roof and looking up at the night sky, I wondered if heaven really was up there somewhere. No one knew—except people who had died . . .

The cold air was spiced with the scent of wood burning from all the chimneys in the small town. I stood there for a moment, looking up at the scattered stars winking behind a few gathering clouds. When I glanced back into the closet, a wonderful idea came to me. Why not bring the angel tree up here? Heaven could use a Christmas tree, couldn't it? Pushing the snow away from the edge of the trap door, I knelt and pulled the blanket off the bush. I spread the scratchy material on the snowy roof, then lay down on my belly and reached for the angel tree. Barely able to touch the branches, I stretched farther down.

I finally caught a firm hold on a strong limb and slowly pulled until I had hefted the bush onto the roof. The electrical cord trailed behind. Relieved, I rolled back on the blanket next to the angel tree, blowing puffs of frosty air into the night.

After a moment I stood up, pulled the blanket around my shoulders, and walked to the edge of the roof. I sat down, hugging my legs to my body to keep warm and staring at the angel tree and the shepherd staff Annie had placed on it. The tree belonged up here with the stars, watching over the Nativity where Annie hoped the baby Jesus would come. And He would—tonight at midnight.

I knew I needed to go back inside. Mom wanted me to be with her and Annie, and I would be in a minute. As I looked down at the island intersection, a yawn caught me. My head suddenly felt very heavy, and a deep tiredness settled over me, making me want to rest my head on my knees. I'd close my eyes for just a moment . . . In just a moment I'd go inside.

POP BOTTLES

I awoke with a start. Blinking and shivering, it took me a moment to figure out why I was on the roof. When I remembered, I quickly checked the Nativity below. Positioned high on the main post of the stable was a new addition: an angel smiling down on the hay-filled manger.

But no baby Jesus yet.

However, a strange red glow was coming from the front of the building.

Leaning way over the edge of the roof, I saw two paramedics loading a gurney into an ambulance. Annie was on it. She lay so still. Mom climbed into the vehicle after the gurney before the paramedics closed the doors.

"Wait!" I yelled. Rushing to the roof's trapdoor, I jumped into the closet, scrambled down the stairs, and burst out onto the sidewalk as the ambulance and the sheriff's car sped away.

Intent on catching them, I charged down the icy street. I ran with everything I had, chasing the fading lights of the ambulance. Even after they disappeared, I kept running.

Pain burned in my side, almost doubling me over. But I kept going, sucking cold air in and out of my lungs until I thought they would burst. After what felt like miles, I finally stopped.

"Annie!" Tears welled up in my eyes. "Mom said you were getting better," I whispered. Wiping my cheeks with the back of my hand, I looked around. Where was I? Across the road was a large field. Piles of tires peeked from beneath the snow, and wayward newspapers tumbled from mounds of snow-covered junk. As I scanned the area, I realized that a lot more garbage lay hidden beneath the white blanket of snow. I'd ended up at the dump.

As I started to walk away, I kicked up a pop bottle hidden beneath the snow. In a flash, I remembered what Wolfgang had said. He earned money by collecting pop bottles from the dump. His stash had to be hidden somewhere around here. And if I found it, I could cash it in. Then I could buy a baby Jesus doll for Annie—one she could have for her very own.

I clung to my new plan like a lifeline. Everything was going to be all right. I'd buy the doll, and Annie would pull through.

Frantically, I began digging through the piles. The snow was cold on my bare hands, but I kept digging. The bottles had to be here somewhere.

Panicked, I ran from pile to pile, kicking snow away and finding only garbage bags. Smells of rotting food and other unidentifiable stenches gagged me. Every once in a while, I caught a glimpse of a furry creature as it scurried over the snow, seeking cover in the debris.

Finally, under a snow-covered tarp that looked vaguely familiar, I found them. Hundreds of pop bottles. I couldn't possibly carry as many as I needed, so I began stuffing some inside my jacket. The glass was cold against my body as I slid the bottles under my arm.

All of a sudden, I felt a hand press down on my shoulder.

"Looking for something, gambler?"

THE NATIVITY BUILDER

I dropped the bottles and turned, raising my fists, ready for a fight.

"Need some bottles?" Wolfgang cleared his throat.

"Yes," I said. I could barely see the shadows of the old man's face, but I could sure smell the odor of onion and garlic. "And I'm taking them. You can't stop me." I started picking up the bottles I'd dropped, stuffing them back inside my coat.

"If you want them, they're yours, but I'm wondering what you're doing here when you should be with your little sister. She needs you now." Wolfgang stood there, not moving.

All the anger and guilt I'd been carrying pressed down on me. How dare this old man try to make me feel worse than I already did. He had no idea how much I wished I was with my little sister.

"You're just a dumb old tramp who lives in the garbage. You don't know what Annie needs. You don't even know where she is." Feeling overwhelmed, I dropped the bottles again.

"Where is she, Micah?" Wolfgang asked softly.

"I don't know." A knot formed in my throat. My eyes stung. How could I explain to him that my sister had just been carted off to some hospital. How could I tell him she was so sick she might die?

My insides were ready to burst. I fell to my knees beside the bottles, feeling totally helpless and abandoned. My stomach knotted up as shivers flashed over my skin. I tried to hold back the words, but I couldn't. "She's dying, and I can't help her." The flood of tears I'd held inside for days, for months, began to escape.

"That's it. Let it out. Let the whole world hear. Get rid of it." Wolfgang stroked the top of my head. "Darned if it doesn't hurt. The ugliness in this world just piles up sometimes, like this dump. You can't just keep takin' and takin'. You've got to let it out, boy."

"I'm sorry," I choked out between sobs. "I shouldn't be stealing your bottles. I'm not a thief, but . . ."

"Come on." Wolfgang motioned to me. "I'm taking you to my home. It's around that trash heap. When I heard somebody out here, I called the sheriff. Need to call him back, tell him not to come. Thought you was that Larken kid. A couple days ago, Sheriff Anderson asked me to call him if Ledge showed up here."

I rubbed my wet hands on my pants and then stood. Sniffing and wiping my nose on the worn cuff of my sleeve, I followed Wolfgang through the snow to his patched-together hut.

"You have a phone?" I asked.

Wolfgang cleaned the snow off his feet on a frayed doormat. "Sure. Sheriff Anderson insisted. A lot of strange things happen at a dump, and he wanted me to be able to call him. He also made a deal with the electric company so I'd have lights." The door to Wolfgang's home was made of old, warped boards nailed together. In the center of the door was a bull's-eye target.

"Make yourself at home." Wolfgang closed the door and latched it with rope. "I'll just be a minute."

A small heater blew warm, soothing air into the room as I studied my surroundings. A makeshift couch constructed of tires and wood slabs sat on the ground. Green, stain-spotted velour curtains had been draped across the middle of the couch. Magazines—mostly medical, it seemed—were stacked in piles all over. On the dirt floor was a braided rug half unraveled, and in the corner was an old traveling trunk. A wall of neatly stacked empty soup cans divided the kitchen and living area.

Against another wall was a table with a red satin tablecloth. Framed pictures had been arranged on top of it. One photograph showed a beautiful little girl with jet-black hair and coal-dark eyes. Her arms were wrapped around a tabby cat, and she was laughing.

Another picture showed the same little girl with a beautiful woman. The woman also had long black hair, which hung to her waist. She and the little girl were swinging in a park that I didn't recognize.

"Make sure you place Him proper in that manger. The baby Jesus' arrival means a lot to everyone in this town." Wolfgang seemed to be warning me. "You're doing this favor not only for me, but for Annie as well." Then the old tramp, who was really a doctor, turned and answered the door.

AN ANGEL ON MAIN STREET

"What's so urgent?" Sheriff Anderson filled the doorway. "I'm needed elsewhere."

"I know." Wolfgang took a deep breath. "Did they take the little girl to the Pocatello hospital?"

"Yes," Sheriff Anderson replied, looking perplexed.

"You need to take me to her, and Micah needs a lift into town."

"Micah's here?" The sheriff ducked to clear the top of the doorway and walked into the hut. "I've been looking all over town for this kid!" He glared at me and then turned back to Wolfgang. "And why do you need to go to the hospital?"

Wolfgang hesitated just a moment and then said, "In my old life, I was a doctor. I promised the boy I'd try to help his sister." He looked up at the confused sheriff. "It's a long story. I can explain on the way." Wolfgang went to the ancient traveling trunk and opened it. After rummaging around for a few moments, he pulled out his framed diploma from Harvard. "Let's go," he said, grabbing his coat.

"But . . ." Sheriff Anderson looked from me to Wolfgang and then muttered, "All right," and turned toward the door.

All at once I realized I couldn't go through with my plan to keep the doll. Wolfgang was right. Annie would want everyone to enjoy the baby Jesus. "I can find my own way back to town," I said. If they took the time to drop me off, it would steal precious minutes that Wolfgang could spend helping Annie. "Please go now."

Sheriff Anderson looked back at me, and his eyes rested on the bundle in my arms. I held the baby Jesus concealed under the burlap as if He were a football instead of an infant, not wanting the sheriff to suspect anything. I braced myself for his questions, but they didn't come.

Before heading out the door, Wolfgang stopped in front of me. "The sheriff will be in touch to let you know what's going on. Pray, Micah. Only the Lord can help us now."

And then they were gone.

As I turned off the heater and lights in Wolfgang's hut, I couldn't help but wonder why Sheriff Anderson hadn't questioned me about the bundle. He hadn't even questioned Wolfgang. He'd just gone along with everything as if he'd known what needed to be done.

I closed the door and trudged out into the snow, taking a last look back at the lonely hut. Who would have thought a doctor lived there? Who would have thought that Wolfgang was the Nativity maker? And why would he want to do something so kind for the town that had treated him so badly?

Then another thought hit me. Had Wolfgang been guided to make the Christmas scene so I would find out he was the Nativity maker and a doctor?

If that were true, it would mean there was more to the Bible than just feel-good stories. And if the Bible were true, it would mean there really was a God watching over everyone. But that couldn't be—it didn't make sense. How could God have taken my father away from me, away from Mom and Annie?

My thoughts swam with unanswered questions. I was getting all mixed up thinking about everything. I needed to focus on getting the baby Jesus to town and doing what I'd promised Wolfgang. I noticed that big snowflakes were floating lazily down from the sky.

As I pulled the collar of Dad's jacket up to my ears, I finally saw the lights of Bolton. I nervously patted the bundle, wondering if Wolfgang and the sheriff had reached the hospital in Pocatello yet. I'd been walking for quite a while, long enough for them to reach the big city ten miles away.

Surely they had arrived.

Surely Wolfgang was helping Annie right this very minute.

I remembered what Wolfgang had said just before he'd left. *Pray, Micah. Only the Lord can help us now.* I didn't know if I could pray. It had been so long; God probably wouldn't listen to me.

Pausing a moment, I took a few deep breaths.

I looked up at the night sky. Staring up at the enormous heavens above was humbling. Snowflakes landed on my face, making me close my eyes. "God, I know you haven't heard from me in a very long time, and you've probably forgotten all about me, but I'm not praying for myself. I'm praying for my friend Wolfgang. See, he's really not a tramp; he's a doctor, and he hasn't worked in a long time, but he knows an awful lot. And I don't think it was a coincidence that I ended up at the dump tonight. See . . . I think somehow You guided me there." I glanced down at the bundle in my arms, at the baby Jesus. Then I looked back up.

"I know You guided me there. And my little sister, Annie, well, she really needs Wolfgang's help right now. She might be dying, and she really believes in You—and Him." I held the bundle out in case God was watching. "She doesn't know Wolfgang, but You do. You know he's studied Annie's sickness, because Wolfgang's little girl died of it and is with You now."

I thought of my father and peered up at the heavens. "My dad is with You, too, so You really don't need my little sister." Closing my eyes to fight back tears, I continued. "And Mom and I need her here with us. If You can please help Wolfgang, I know he can save Annie. I just know he can. But You see, Wolfgang doesn't know this. Please help him know what to do. Please."

I slowly opened my eyes. I hoped I'd done it right. Then, brushing the snow from my face, I continued my journey to town. As I walked down Main Street, the only sound I heard was the muted thud of my sneakers on the fallen snow. Everyone was at home with their loved ones, celebrating Christmas Eve. Glancing up at the courthouse clock, I saw it was almost midnight. The flashing red stoplight over the intersection island lit my way through the flurry of snowflakes wafting down through the night.

As I approached the island, I thought of the Nativity snow globe Wolfgang had given his daughter. I felt as if I'd stepped inside it as snowflakes swirled around me and the figurines. Looking at Joseph, I couldn't shake the feeling that the statue was staring at me. Nervously, I shifted my gaze to the wise men and shepherds. Were they watching too? I hesitated and listened.

No noise. No cars. Just quiet.

I was suddenly filled with a sense of reverence, as if what I was about to do was sacred. I looked at the statue of Mary. Her eyes shone on the empty manger filled with hay.

Laying the bundle down, I pulled the burlap bag away from the baby.

The infant was smiling. Not a funny, laughing smile, but a patient, caring one. I glanced back at Mary and blinked. A more contented look seemed to grace her eyes. I shook my head, sure that the cold was getting to me.

I looked at the infant. My mission was accomplished; I could tell Annie that the baby Jesus had arrived.

As I was about to turn and leave, I was suddenly overcome by a warm, comforting feeling. It seemed to start inside of me and wash over my skin. The peaceful feeling grew stronger and stronger. I quickly glanced down, sure I must be glowing. I wasn't, but the feeling continued.

When I looked back at the baby Jesus, I saw an adult hand holding something small and shining, reaching toward the infant. I held my breath; a grapefruit-sized lump formed in my throat. My gaze trailed up the arm to the face of the personage standing beside me.

There, holding the shepherd's crook Annie had made for the baby Jesus, stood my dad.

Radiance glowed about his kind, craggy face, and his white robes were bathed in light; Dad's entire being appeared to be lit from within. I blinked hard, trying to focus, trying to understand whether this was really happening. I briefly wondered whether I'd fallen down and was unconscious somewhere between Bolton and the dump. But whatever had happened, I didn't want the bubble to burst and take my father away from me . . . again.

His auburn hair, which had been graying at his temples when he'd left for Korea, was parted on the right side like I remembered, but the gray was gone. His cheeks had a healthy, rosy shine, and his eyes sparkled as though reflecting heavenly light. When he smiled, any doubts about whether this man could really be my father vanished.

Dad placed the little staff Annie had made in baby Jesus' hand. I recognized the grace of my father's movements. Long ago, I'd watched him as he mastered the gentle touch of a true carpenter, making the finishing touches to Mom's beloved rocking chair down in the basement of our Boise apartment building. I quickly glanced at the back of his hand, searching for a trace of the ugly scar I'd made when I had accidentally dropped a chisel on his calloused knuckles. At first I couldn't see it, but then a flash of it appeared as a thin, trailing scar. And then it was gone. He smiled at me again, and I knew he understood my doubts—and that he needed me to believe.

"Son . . ." The familiar husky tone of my father's bass voice stirred a renewed sense of faith in me. I hadn't heard him speak for so very long and desperately hoped he would continue.

I yearned to run and throw my arms around him, but I was afraid that if I so much as moved he'd disappear. Then I remembered Annie. I was filled with an urgent need to tell Dad what was going on with my little sister.

"Annie's really sick. She might die, and I can't do anything to help her."

"You found the only man who could. Go to your mom, Micah. She needs you." Dad started to slowly back away from me.

Panicked, I cried, "Don't go! You have to help her. You have to help Annie!"

He seemed reluctant to leave but kept moving just the same, a sympathetic glint in his chocolate-colored eyes that were so much like my little sister's.

"Take me with you." I begged, slapping away the tears that had escaped down my cheeks. "Dad . . ." I had just taken a step after him when suddenly the courthouse clock began to chime its twelve o'clock melody, welcoming Christmas Day. Startled, I glanced at the clock, and when I turned back, my father was gone.

A trembling overtook me as I tried to understand and believe what had happened.

I quickly scanned the area. Maybe I'd mistaken him for one of the shepherds. But all I saw was the snow fluttering around me, and all I heard was silence. A sliver of doubt pricked me. Maybe he was never here at all.

My eyes were drawn to the manger. The red stoplight overhead shone down on the doll in a rosy glow and hit the tinfoil shepherd's staff resting in baby Jesus' hand.

Quiet, so quiet. Snowflakes fluttered around me as my heart hammered against my ribs 'til I thought my chest would burst. My head felt light and dizzy. As I gazed on Jesus' face, I felt as if I were being pulled back in time, becoming part of the Nativity. Standing there on Main Street in Bolton, Idaho, the miracle that had taken place in Bethlehem could not have been more real to me had I heard the herald angels sing and gazed upon the real infant Christ sent to save the world. A sure knowledge sprang up in my heart. He had been born in a lowly stable. Over two thousand years ago, He had come to earth, lived, and died to save mankind—all mankind . . . even me.

My skin prickled with gooseflesh.

At that moment, a strong hand patted my shoulder. I jumped and turned about, hoping against hope that my father had returned. Instead, I saw that Sheriff Anderson stood where Dad had stood. Gasping for breath and more than a little disappointed, I looked up at the giant of a man, unable to speak.

My bottom lip trembled. Biting my lips together, I glanced down at the shepherd's crook in baby Jesus' hand, then back up at the sheriff.

Finding my voice, I softly said, "I didn't put that there." I swallowed past the hard, prickly lump in my throat.

"Who did?" The sheriff's voice was calm and thoughtful.

"My father." I bit my lip to fight the tears that threatened to form in my eyes.

The sheriff rubbed his chin. As he studied the baby Jesus, his face took on a solemn, yet knowing expression. "You saw your dad, didn't you?"

Nodding, I studied the sheriff's strong face. I had said such mean things to this man, accusing him of trying to steal my mom and sister from me and of trying to weasel his way into our lives. After all this, could it be that Sheriff Garth Anderson believed me? I glanced at Joseph and Mary as if they could confirm my suspicion, but they continued staring serenely at the baby Jesus. I looked up at the sheriff, waiting for him to say something more.

He cleared his throat and said, "There aren't many people at the hospital this time of night. I think I can safely sneak you in." Then he took my hand in his, squeezed, and said, "Let's go see how Annie's doing."

So there would be no probing questions, no meddling with what was sacred. He was leaving it up to me, letting me decide what I would share. I squeezed his hand back. Someday I'd tell him what had just happened . . . someday I'd tell him everything. But not right now.

* * *

The ride to the hospital took forever. I leaned my forehead on the car's cold window, thinking about everything that had happened that night. Once again, I was filled with wonder. *I had seen my dad.*

He'd said that I had found the only man who could help Annie. As I thought about this, I marveled at how everything had come together. I remembered how suddenly I'd fallen asleep on the roof—causing me to miss the ambulance, chase after it, and end up at the dump. I'd had every intention of minding Mom's request to come back inside. I knew my falling asleep had been no accident.

Sheriff Anderson tugged on my arm. I'd been so deep in thought that I hadn't realized we'd arrived at the hospital.

"Let's go in." The sheriff climbed out of the car, and I chased after him.

The place seemed empty except for a few nurses who looked my way, probably concerned that a kid under twelve had been allowed in. But they left me alone because I was with the sheriff.

We took the elevator to the fourth floor. Sheriff Anderson guided me to a door with a sign that read ICU.

"I'll go in and see what's going on." The sheriff gave me a pat on the back. "Sit on the couch over there. If anyone gives you trouble, tell them you're with me."

He disappeared behind the door, and I wandered over to the couch. A little Christmas tree had been placed in the corner. Funny-looking paper ornaments, probably made by children in the ICU, hung on its branches. I spied a shepherd's staff and smiled. Then, slumping down on the couch, I settled in to wait for the sheriff. But the minutes ticked by and soon, despite my worry, I was asleep.

When I awoke it was morning. The halls were filled with busy doctors and nurses hustling up and down the hallways. I rubbed my eyes, confused. The sheriff had said he'd just be a minute.

What was taking so long? Was Annie okay? Then I remembered what had happened the night before at the Nativity. I took a deep breath and sat back against the couch, comforted by the memory.

The ICU door opened, and an old man in surgical scrubs walked out. His long gray hair was combed back into a ponytail. He looked at me, and despite his clean, well-groomed appearance, I knew immediately who he was.

"Hey, gambler!" Wolfgang smiled.

"Annie—is she all right?"

Wolfgang squatted down next to me. "She's going to be fine."

I was so full of joy that I leaped at Wolfgang, and we both fell to the floor laughing. After a moment, the old man stood and pulled me to my feet.

"I knew you could do it." I hugged my friend.

"Did you do everything I asked you to do?" Wolfgang questioned, looking down on me.

At first I didn't know what he was talking about. Then I understood. "Yes. The baby Jesus is in the manger." I smiled, proud of what I'd done.

"And you must have prayed," Wolfgang said as he studied my eyes, searching for the truth.

I nodded, unable to speak.

"That's what I thought." He put his arm around my shoulders. "I think it's time you go see your little sister. She's awake and asking for you."

I reached for the door and stopped. "Is it all right? Will the nurses let me see her?"

"I don't think they'd dare stop you." Wolfgang gave me a friendly nudge just as the door opened and Mom and Sheriff Anderson walked out.

As soon as she saw me, Mom rushed to me and threw her arms around my neck. "She's going to be fine. Isn't it a miracle?"

I couldn't talk, because I knew I'd just cry. Mom continued. "Wolfgang said he came because of you. Your dad would be so proud!" She wiped the tears from her eyes. "Let's go in and see Annie."

"Can I go alone?" I asked, hoping I wouldn't hurt Mom's feelings. I didn't want anyone with me when I told Annie about what had happened the night before. This was something I thought should stay between me and her for a little while.

Sheriff Anderson took Mom's hand. "Let him go in, Dawn." He winked at me, and I knew he understood.

"Of course. We'll be waiting." Mom kissed my cheek. I gave her a hug and then pushed open the door to the ICU.

There were five rooms along the hallway. In the first was an old man with all sorts of machines hooked up to him. In the next was a young boy. His parents sat beside his bed, gazing at their son. Prayers were written across their faces.

The next room was Annie's. She lay on her back in bed, an IV hooked up to her arm. Her eyes were closed, and for a second I started to worry. Then I saw her eyes flutter open as she looked at me.

"Micah." Her voice was just a whisper.

"Hey, Annie Bananie!"

"You promised you wouldn't call me that anymore." She weakly pretended to pout.

I smiled. "You like it, and you know you do. Guess who's in the manger?" I couldn't wait to see her reaction.

But I didn't see the surprised look on her face I'd been expecting.

"I know," she said softly, smiling at me.

"You don't know." I rubbed her small arm, careful of the IV needle.

"Yes, I do." She blinked, then gazed at me intently.

"How do you know?"

"Daddy told me you put the baby Jesus in the manger."

Goosebumps skittered over my arms and down my spine. "You saw Dad, too."

"Yes." Annie smiled as tears filled her eyes.

Then I felt it: the pounding of my heart. Annie had told me that when she felt her heart pounding, she knew that God was watching over her and that everything would be all right. She had known it all along. Now I knew it too.

ABOUT THE AUTHOR

Born in Rigby, Idaho, Kathi Oram Peterson knows how fortunate she was to grow up in a small town during the fifties, when Santa Claus arrived on the local fire engine, Christmas trees were a dollar a foot, and the Nativity was revered by all. Kathi has long since grown up, married, and had a family. Once her children were grown, she returned to college and earned her English degree at the University of Utah. Upon graduation, she worked for a curriculum publisher writing and editing children's concept and biography books. After leaving the workforce, she turned her attention to writing inspirational fiction and children's books. Of the many stories she has written, *An Angel on Main Street* will always remain one of her favorites. You can contact Kathi through her Web site: www.kathiorampeterson.com.